"Careful, Simo
narrowed. A n
"Swearing doe

"If you had any kind of memory left, you'd remember that I often take exquisite pleasure in *not* behaving like a lady. Would you like a demonstration?"

"What are you going to do, Princess?" They were toe-to-toe. Tension radiated from him in waves. "Hit me?"

"Oh, no." Tempting as it was. "I was thinking of something a whole lot more subtle by way of a demonstration." She put her hand to his chest, to his heart, before finally curving it round the back of his neck and pressing her lips to the strong curve of his jaw. Gently.

"You think I didn't love you," she murmured. Another kiss for that stubborn jaw, followed by the slow slide of her lips across to the edge of his mouth. "You think your feelings were the stronger."

She gave him time to move away. She did give him that.

His chest heaved and he drew a ragged breath. But he stayed right where he was.

"You're wrong," she whispered, and she set her lips to his.

His lips were warm and firm. And closed. She touched the tip of her tongue to the crease in them and tasted salt. She felt the shudder that ripped through him but his mouth stayed stubbornly closed to her. She started to pull away. Experiment over. Experiment failed.

And then his hand came up to cup her face, his lips opened beneath hers, a dam broke somewhere and the world around her simply disappeared.

Dear Presents Reader,

Spring has definitely sprung, and with it everywhere is bursting with fresh new beginnings and vibrant color. Every month there are two books that offer you all you expect from Harlequin Presents, but with fresh, vibrant, sparkling new voices—and a sexy, young, flirty attitude! From next month, you'll find these stories in Presents Extra, available two weeks later than the usual Harlequin Presents series.

These exciting new books are written by an array of bright, spirited authors such as Kate Hardy, Robyn Grady, Natalie Anderson, Heidi Rice, Lucy King, Anne Oliver, Kelly Hunter and Anna Cleary. This month, don't miss the final installment of Kelly Hunter's duet HOT BED OF SCANDAL, *Revealed: A Prince and a Pregnancy.* And when artist Didi O'Flanagan accepts a commission of a lifetime, she's sucked into a hedonistic life of glamour and luxury in *Memoirs of a Millionaire's Mistress* by Anne Oliver.

Next month, both heroines need financial investment from the heroes. Can they keep their relationships STRICTLY BUSINESS? Find out in these sexy, sparky stories: *Hot Boss, Boardroom Mistress* by Natalie Anderson and *Good Girl or Gold-Digger?* by Kate Hardy. Look out for these in Presents Extra, on sale May 11, 2010.

We'd love to hear what you think of these novels— why not drop us a line at Presents@hmb.co.uk.

With best wishes,

The editors

Kelly Hunter

REVEALED: A PRINCE AND A PREGNANCY

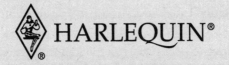

HARLEQUIN®

TORONTO • NEW YORK • LONDON
AMSTERDAM • PARIS • SYDNEY • HAMBURG
STOCKHOLM • ATHENS • TOKYO • MILAN • MADRID
PRAGUE • WARSAW • BUDAPEST • AUCKLAND

Recycling programs
for this product may
not exist in your area.

ISBN-13: 978-0-373-12913-3

REVEALED: A PRINCE AND A PREGNANCY

First North American Publication 2010.

Copyright © 2009 by Kelly Hunter.

All about the author...
Kelly Hunter

Accidentally educated in the sciences, **KELLY HUNTER** has always had a weakness for fairy tales, fantasy worlds and losing herself in a good book. Husband... yes. Children...two boys. Cooking and cleaning...sigh. Sports...no, not really, in spite of the best efforts of her family. Gardening...yes—roses, of course. Kelly was born in Australia and has traveled extensively. Although she enjoys living and working in different parts of the world, she still calls Australia home.

Visit Kelly online at www.kellyhunter.net

Two families, torn apart by secrets and desire, are about to be reunited in
Hot Bed of Scandal
a sexy new duet by Kelly Hunter from
Harlequin Presents®!

Exposed: Misbehaving with the Magnate—
March 2010

Gabriella Alexander returns to the French vineyard she was banished from, after being caught in flagrante with the owner's son Lucien Duvalier—only to finish what they started!

Revealed: A Prince and a Pregnancy—April 2010

Simone Duvalier wants Rafael Alexander and always has, but they both get more than they bargained for when a night of passion and a royal revelation rock their world!

Don't miss this sassy duet!

Available wherever Harlequin Presents is sold.

**To Maytoners.
And Puppies.**

CHAPTER ONE

THE moment she saw the elegant two-storey guest house nestled in the heart of one of Australia's premier winegrowing regions, Simone Duvalier approved of it. Granted, it was no seventeenth-century French chateau, but if one *had* to attend a wedding halfway around the world then this picturesque venue gave at least some consolation. Someone here had an eye for detail, reflected in the immaculately kept gardens and gleaming house. Someone here had a penchant for whimsy. The strutting metal flamingos cobbled together from nuts and bolts and what looked like spare engine parts telegraphed that.

As for the scenery… The big sky and the eucalypt-clad hills on the horizon. The tidy rows of grapevines flanking the drive… She'd been expecting a hint of wildness about the Australian landscape and it did not disappoint her, but there was order here too and that surprised her. Simone liked surprises. Surprise was an emotion that could almost compete with the nervousness that clawed through her whenever she thought about seeing Rafael Alexander again.

Rafael, her childhood playmate. Rafael, the house-keeper's son.

Rafe the ambitious, the driven, the brilliant.

Rafael, the man she'd spurned.

Would he hold a grudge? Still? After almost nine years?

Would her soon-to-be brother-in-law be in *any* way pleased to see her? Probably not, but the one thing she'd made sure he could not do was throw her out. The land surrounding the guest house might have belonged to Rafael, but the guest house itself did not. And as adamant as Gabrielle had been about the wedding taking place in Australia rather than France, she'd also chosen to hold both the ceremony and the reception here at the guest house rather than at Rafe's vineyard.

Neutral ground, and a concession for which Simone was supremely grateful.

Smiling grimly, Simone negotiated the narrow driveway and parked her hired Audi in the car park behind the guest house before finally cutting the engine. At least she had a day to compose herself before meeting him again. Time enough to recover from her flight and the harrowing drive to the valley. Time enough for her to put on her happy face and work her way in to the moment.

'One step at a time,' she murmured. That was how she'd made it this far. By forcing one foot in front of the other, painting a smile on her face and making herself move towards the moment she dreaded.

Courage, mon ami, Gabrielle had whispered when she'd told Simone that the wedding would be held in Australia and that Rafael had agreed to stand as Luc's best man.

Courage, when every instinct screamed at Simone to forgo her bridesmaid duties and run.

But Gabrielle had been adamant. *It's time you faced him again. It's time he faced you.*

Courage.

So here she was. Finally setting foot in Australia. Finally about to confront the ghosts of her past, for better or for worse. But not quite yet. Tomorrow would be plenty soon enough. For now, all she needed was her overnight bag, her car keys, Gabrielle's gown and a room. Lord, let there be room at the inn. Simone had deliberately neglected to notify *anyone* of her early arrival and that included the guest-house staff.

The entrance foyer to the guest house was decorated in the French provincial style, albeit with some strikingly Australian floral arrangements. The young receptionist behind the desk smiled cheerfully, her eyes widening as she took in the garment bag draped over Simone's arm. 'Uh oh,' she muttered as she hurried around the counter to take, not the garment bag, but Simone's overnight case and car keys. 'You're Simone Duvalier. We weren't expecting you until tomorrow.'

'I know. But there was a slight change of flight plans. I come in heartfelt hope that you might have a room available for me tonight.'

'You've just flown in from Paris and driven here?' asked the girl, and at her nod, 'No wonder you look exhausted! But you're in luck. I prepped your room earlier this morning, though I haven't cut your flowers yet.' She motioned for Simone to follow her along a hallway leading off from the foyer. 'I'll get you some later this afternoon, once the sun's gone off them.'

'You cut flowers from the garden outside?' asked Simone, intrigued, as she followed the young woman along the wide hallway with its polished wooden floors and pressed metal ceilings.

'As often as we can, yes. Want to come with me

later? A lot of our guests enjoy picking out the flowers they'd like.'

'I'm sure they do,' said Simone, charmed. 'How do you stop guests from choosing blooms that you don't want cut?'

'Easy,' said the girl and glanced back at Simone with a dimpled smile. 'I say "No, not that one." Works a treat.'

'I'm sure it does.' Simone smiled her bemusement. She'd heard these Australians were a sunny people, given to irreverence and informality. She just hadn't realised quite how unselfconsciously they served it up.

The room the receptionist took her to was feminine and airy, with a secluded courtyard and a separate dining area. The receptionist set Simone's overnight case on the luggage rack, peeled back curtains and crossed to a large set of white louvre doors, opening them wide to reveal a walk-in wardrobe. Lemon-scented white linen sheets had been laid over gleaming wooden floorboards and a dressmaker's dummy stood in the centre of the sheets, naked and waiting.

'Gaby mentioned that you'd be bringing her wedding dress with you. Will this do for somewhere to put it?'

'Perfect,' said Simone. 'The couturiers at Yves St Laurent would most definitely approve.'

'Yves St Laurent?' The girl eyed the garment bag in Simone's arms with unabashed curiosity. 'Gaby didn't mention *that*. She's wearing an Yves St Laurent wedding dress?'

'*Oui*. And as soon as I shower and change into clean clothes I will call for you and we shall set the gown in place on the dressmaker's bodice. Then we shall call the bride-to-be over to see what she thinks of it, yes?'

'Yes,' said the girl with another dimpled smile as Simone carefully laid the gown on the bed for now.

'Ask for Sarah. Sarah who loves her job.' With one last glance towards the garment bag, the girl collected herself and dangled Simone's rental car keys from her fingers. 'I'll bring the rest of your luggage in.'

'Thank you. Oh, and there are half a dozen cases of champagne in the rear of the car.' She'd hauled them all the way from Caverness—thank heaven for porters—and the sooner she was free of them, the better. 'Could you see that they come in as well?'

'No problem. Where do you want them?'

'I don't suppose you have a dedicated drinks cool room operating at four degrees Celsius on hand?'

'You're in the heart of vineyard country. Of course we do.'

Of course they did. Simone was well on her way to falling in love with this fine establishment.

Sarah, who loved her job, jiggled the car keys and headed for the door. 'I'll send one of the cellar staff over with a receipt for your champagne. The receipt tells you exactly where we've stored it. When you want the champagne back just hand someone the receipt.'

'It's for Gabrielle's wedding toasts. I believe the reception is to be held at the restaurant here on Sunday?'

Sarah nodded.

'Then perhaps you could notify the maître d' of the champagne's arrival and location as well?'

'Will do.' Sarah left.

Simone waited until Sarah had closed the door behind her before crossing to her overnight case, retrieving her toiletries and heading for the bathroom, a white-on-grey marble affair with plush towels and stage-mirror lighting. 'Oh, yes,' she murmured. This place was just full of surprises. 'I could get very fond of *you.*'

She'd been born into wealth, lots of it, and the family fortune had only risen over the years, but that didn't mean Simone took her wealth or the benefits that came with it for granted. It was her *duty* to appreciate the finer things in life, and appreciate them she did.

Long minutes later, Simone emerged from the steamy shower cubicle and reached for a fluffy white towel. She'd barely finished drying her hair before a hammering noise started up at the door to her suite.

Cellar staff, Sarah had said. Impatient cellar staff.

'Wait,' she muttered, tucking the towel around her body and heading for the door, making sure she stood well behind it before opening it a fraction and peering out.

Not cellar staff, though he looked the part in his battered boots and well-worn work trousers. His grey T-shirt had seen better days too and could have been shapeless if not for the aid of the superbly muscled chest beneath it. His face was one she saw in her dreams, a strong and impossibly handsome face. Beloved once. Beautiful still. In her dreams those vivid blue eyes were always laughing, inviting her to share the joke and the moment with him. They weren't laughing now.

'Your receipt,' he said quietly, and held it up between long strong fingers. 'I was delivering the red wine for the wedding when the champagne came in.'

She opened the door a fraction wider and took the slip of paper from him. Their fingers did not touch. Rafael's eyes did not warm. Not a dream then, but awkward, uncomfortable reality. *'Merci.'*

'You're early,' he said next.

'Yes.' What could she say? That she'd arrived a day early so as to avoid having Gabrielle—or him—meet her at the airport? That she'd taken that extra time deliberately in order to armour herself against seeing him again? 'Yes. A little early.'

Rafe's eyes narrowed as he searched her face. 'May I come in?'

'No!' Too breathless. Far too hasty. 'No,' she said again, trying for more composure. 'Now's not a good time.'

His eyed hardened. 'I'm sorry. I didn't realise you had company.'

Company? *Company?* As if she would attend this particular wedding with a lover in tow. Cursing herself for a fool, she moved out from behind the door and swung it wide open so that he could see for himself the kind of company she kept. Rafe's hard gaze swept the room before returning to clash with hers.

Day, the household staff had named him back when they were children and Rafe had called Caverness home. Day, because of the sunshine in his nature and the brightness of his smile, never mind that he'd been the housekeeper's unloved and unwanted son. And Lucien—her brother and Rafe's partner in crime— Lucien with his watchful ways and inky-black hair had been Night. Somehow, it seemed as if their roles had been reversed.

'I'm a little underdressed at the moment.' Meeting him bereft of make-up and clad only in a towel had *not* been part of her master plan. 'So if you would be so good as to *leave…*'

'Being good isn't something I excel at,' he murmured silkily and leaned against the doorway, all raw and powerful male. His eyes made a leisurely study of her person. 'Nice towel.'

He was fabulous when he was bad. She hadn't forgotten. 'Still out to defy the world, I see? How…predictable.'

'No, I've given up defying the world. The reasoning

was flawed.' He sent her a devil's smile. 'Now I just want to rule it.'

'Mmm.' She sent him as cool a stare as she could manage for a woman dressed in a towel. 'Wouldn't a psychiatrist have fun with *you*.'

'Well, she *could*,' he murmured. 'But only if she were naked and willing to be a very bad girl.'

Simone's breath hitched in her throat and she could have sworn a flush started in the vicinity of her toes and shot straight to her scalp.

'She could analyse herself afterwards,' he continued in that dark, delicious rumble. 'Give her something to do with her time because there certainly wouldn't be any challenge in analysing me. I'm a simple soul, really.'

Not from where she was standing. Simone could feel herself being drawn towards him, moth to flame and perfectly willing to burn for just one more taste of all that barely contained heat.

Her luggage and car keys stood just inside the door. Simone reached for the suitcase handle, determined to stay calm. 'I only arrived a few minutes ago. It'll be ten more before I'm ready to see you,' she murmured, and wished that her voice sounded steadier. She headed for the bathroom fast, grateful that the suitcase she towed behind her had wheels. 'Close the door behind you if you decide not to wait,' she added over her shoulder.

'I'm not your servant, princess.' There was no ignoring the bite in his words. 'And you've *never* been ready for me.'

Finally, she thought with grim satisfaction. *Finally*, an honest reaction from him. 'Yes, well…' She reached down deep and called for calm in the face of his simmering, seething resentment. 'I'll be ten minutes.'

She shut herself in the bathroom, sinking back against the wall as reaction set in. She held her hands out in front of her, palms down to the floor. Shaking hands and a heavy heart at what he could still make her feel, even after all these years. She closed her eyes and breathed deeply, willing strength to her limbs and resolve to her trembling heart.

Time to get dressed. Time to find clothes in her suitcase that lent confidence and poise. Clothes that armed a woman against a man such as Rafael.

Beige trousers and her favourite sleeveless shirt in rich plum colours. Add a pair of vertiginous strappy leather sandals, a Cartier watch and a gauzy rainforest-green silk scarf; run a brush through her hair, emphasise her lips and eyes with a touch of make-up and maybe, just maybe, this time she'd be ready for him.

Not that she ever had been before.

Rafael brooded in silence as he made his way from the guest room into the tiny private courtyard attached to it. Simone Duvalier wasn't meant to be here. Not today. Not ever, if Rafael had any say in the matter. Not that he seemed to have much say in anything of late. His sister's upcoming wedding to Luc Duvalier had seen to that. Why they weren't getting married in France where there was a perfectly serviceable seventeenth-century chateau at their disposal was anyone's guess, but no, Gabrielle had insisted on holding the ceremony in Australia. Which meant that the wedding party entourage—which, granted, consisted only of Luc and Simone—were coming here.

He didn't want them here.

Not Luc, for all that they had retained some semblance of friendship over the years.

Not Simone, looking flustered and fetching and far too vulnerable for his liking.

Rafe scowled at the jasmine climbing its way up the stone courtyard wall. Hadn't he taught her never to appear weak in the face of one's enemies? Hadn't she remembered *any* of the lessons growing up at Caverness had taught them?

Never show fear, especially when your hands were slick with it.

Never let on how much something means to you lest someone take it away.

Never back down. Never give in.

Never look back.

Simone hadn't had to learn that last lesson, only Rafael, but he'd never forgotten it. Indeed, he'd got royally drunk on one of his first nights in Australia and had those exact three words cut into his back. Not that he'd ever *seen* the tattoo, mind, although more than one woman had professed herself captivated by its beauty. Not once, in all the years it had graced his skin, had he ever sought its image.

He *never* looked back.

What the *hell* was taking her so long?

He had a million things to do today. Laying down the law on exactly how Simone Duvalier would conduct herself during her stay here hadn't been one of them. That task had been on his list of things to do *tomorrow*.

Not that that bothered him. Rafael was an opportunist in the purest sense of the word. Today would do just as well. 'Here's how it's going to be,' he would say. 'You're going to stay out of my way. I'm going to stay out of yours. And you will not set foot in my house or on my land during your time here because I don't want you there. Ever. Clear?' And she would say, 'Yes, crystal clear,' with her eyes downcast, at which point he would get the hell out of there before he changed his mind.

Rafe paced the courtyard—he figured this took all of three seconds. He considered he might just probably be climbing the courtyard walls by the time Simone deigned to put in an appearance. How could it *possibly* take her ten minutes to throw on some clothes and run a comb through her hair?

Exactly ten minutes later Simone emerged from the bathroom, a vision of elegant sophistication and poise. She didn't look towards the still open door, no, she turned her head towards the courtyard and looked straight at him, as if she'd known all along that he would be waiting for her there. He felt the impact of that quiet assessing gaze hit him like a silken fist.

She stepped out into the courtyard, one elegantly sandal-clad and perfectly pedicured foot in front of the other. 'I thought we might perhaps manage a greeting this time round, but I can see you're not in the mood,' she said quietly.

He wasn't. And it rankled him mightily that she knew it.

'Would you care for a drink?' she said next. 'I was about to call for some coffee.'

'No.'

'Or, there's probably juice or cola in the fridge if you'd prefer something cold. Come to think of it, I'd prefer something cold. Are you sure I can't get you something?'

She disappeared back inside, leaving Rafe to either follow her, which he would never do, or stay where he was and seethe in silence, which he accomplished effortlessly.

She returned a minute or so later with a tall glass of clear liquid. 'They only had water,' she said. 'I guess you order what you want from room service. That or Sarah will restock the fridge when she does the flowers.'

'We need to set some ground rules,' he told her curtly.

'Not a social visit, then? Who would have guessed?'

Rafael watched in silence as Simone sipped her drink, soft, lush lips to cool, smooth glass. Rafe hadn't been thirsty a moment ago. Now he was parched.

'Am I going to like these ground rules?' she asked next.

'You might,' he offered, dragging his gaze from her lips. Not that he gave a damn whether she liked them or not. 'You might find that they make your stay here easier for all concerned.'

'Ah, yes. The easy road.' She looked around the courtyard, her gaze following the trail of jasmine up and over the wall. 'Why is it, do you think, that the easy road so rarely takes a person where they want to go?'

'It can,' he said. 'It depends where you want to go.'

'Call it a wild hunch, but I don't think we're heading for the same place.' She slanted him a glance, heavy on the doe-eyed innocence. Warning klaxons rang in his brain. Childhood memories surfaced. The ingénue look had usually signalled Simone at her devious best. And Simone at her devious best had been very wily indeed.

'So…about these rules…' she said. 'Am I to stay out of your way as much as possible? Refuse all invitations from Gabrielle to show me the vineyard you restored and made your own? Am I to pretend that our shared history does not exist?'

She knew him too well. He glared at her, but he didn't contradict her. 'It's a start.'

'It's a mistake,' she countered lightly. 'Funny things, boundaries. All they ever seem to do is make a person want to push against them.' Her gaze turned dark and knowing. 'But then…you already know that.'

Just like that, effortlessly and with surgical precision, she cut the ground from beneath him.

'I will not cower in the shadows during my stay here, Rafael.' She stepped closer, too close. 'I will not pretend polite indifference towards you. I reject your rules of engagement. Mine is a different road.'

He could smell the scent on her skin, something delicate and floral and quintessentially French. He was close enough to touch her if he wanted to. And he *did* want to. Not lovingly or gently but in desperation and in need. Slowly, deliberately, he jammed his hands in his pockets and stepped back. 'Yours is a dangerous road.'

'We played together as children,' she said quietly. 'I knew you then. I knew your soul and it wasn't a simple one, but I knew it nonetheless. We loved together in our youth and I felt your dreams and breathed your fears, but duty prevented me from following where you led. Sometimes, when I look back, I regret the choices I've made. And sometimes I don't.'

She looked away then, as if the sight of him hurt her eyes. 'I cannot change our past, Rafael. It happened. It's done. But I can influence the present and I would have us leave the past behind if we could. I want new memories to replace the old. Even bittersweet ones would be better than the ones I carry now.'

She took a shuddering breath. There was fear here; he felt it as if it were his own. Maybe it was. Run, he pleaded silently. Dear God, Simone, don't do this. Don't even try.

'Do you know what I would take from you this visit?' she said quietly. 'Friendship.'

'Don't,' he muttered. 'Simone, *don't*.'

'Guarded if you like. Conditional if need be. But I would very much like to get to know the man you've become.'

'No.' She asked too much of him. She always had. He headed for the door, knowing it for retreat. Knowing that whatever ground he'd thought to protect, he'd somehow just lost. 'I can't walk that road with you,' he said hoarsely. 'Not now, not ever.' He let his anger surface, he let it fan his pain and she flinched away from what she saw in his eyes and well she should have. He headed for the door, fast, before he hauled her in his arms and showed her exactly why he could never be her friend. 'I just can't.'

Simone stood her ground as he strode from the courtyard and then from the room without a backward glance. She knew he wouldn't look back, he never had, even as a boy. Forward was the only way for Rafael and she had hoped to appeal to that need in him. Confront the past head on in order to *move* on.

So much for that particular notion.

Simone closed her eyes and let the twin blades of weariness and abandonment overtake her.

She'd come here for a wedding because she had to. She'd come here, out of her element and out of her league, to try and broker some sort of peace with her past and with Rafael.

She was trying, dammit!

Coffee would be good. Coffee, and then she and Sarah would fit the bridal gown to the dressmaker's dummy and then she would make that call to Gabrielle.

There were jobs to do. Steps to take. She would take pleasure in helping to make Luc and Gabrielle's wedding day a perfect one. She would find joy in the little things. She would not give way to despair.

As for Rafael, with his smouldering gaze and his barely concealed anger…

Courage.

CHAPTER TWO

'IT's exquisite,' said Gabrielle in a hushed and reverent whisper as she fingered the pearl edging of the neckline. 'I knew when they took my measurements and we agreed on a basic design that it'd be lovely, but never in a million years did I imagine a gown as beautiful as this. It's like something from a fairy tale. A very sophisticated French fairy tale,' she added with a grin. 'Wait 'til Lucien sees it!'

'Exactly,' said Simone. 'I trust you've organised hair and make-up assistance for Sunday?'

'Done,' said Gabrielle. 'Oh, Simone, thank you. Thank you for bringing all this with you, and for coming. I know you have your reservations, but I'm so glad you're here.'

'Yes, well…well-founded reservations notwithstanding, I'm glad I'm here too.' She sat back and smiled at Gabrielle's continued fascination with her wedding gown. 'I think we need to get better acquainted with the room service hereabouts. How does a plate full of salmon and black caviar canapés sound? It seems it's on the menu.'

'Do they come with a chilled Semillon Blanc?'

'I'm sure they *could*…' Simone grinned and reached for the phone. 'Let me see.'

Simone added a selection of local cheese and biscuits to the order and replaced the phone in the receiver, well satisfied with her efforts. 'Food and beverage is on the way. What else do bridesmaids usually do?'

'They show the bride their bridesmaid gown.' Gabrielle dragged her gaze away from her wedding dress long enough to spear Simone with a narrow-eyed glance. 'And what do you mean by "well-founded" reservations? You haven't even seen Rafe yet.'

'Not true. He happened by this afternoon.' Simone headed for the outer hanging cupboard and pulled a strapless floor-length gown in coffee cream with slightly darker pearl beading across the bodice from its depths. '*Voila!* It suits me very well and offsets your gown to perfection. I told you the couturier knew what he was doing.'

'And so he should, considering what he charges. But you're right, he does know clothes. You're going to look divine.' Gabrielle sent her a questioning smile. 'Ordinarily I would wax lyrical over the gown a little longer, but my curiosity's killing me. Rafe was here earlier?'

'Mmm-hmm.' Simone slid the dress back into the cupboard and shut the door.

'And?' Gabrielle sounded impatient.

Simone turned to face her. 'And what?'

'Stop stalling. Was he civil?'

'After a fashion.'

'Were *you* civil?'

'But of course,' she said lightly.

'It was a disaster, wasn't it?' asked Gabrielle darkly.

'Yes.'

'Do you still have feelings for him?'

'We grew up together, Gabrielle. I'll always have feelings for him. Nothing can change that.'

'Okay, fair enough, let me rephrase. Do you still desire him?'

Trust Gabrielle to get straight to the heart of the matter. 'It's hard to say.'

'Say it anyway,' muttered Gabrielle. 'Let me rephrase *again*. Does he still want you?'

'He couldn't get away quickly enough,' muttered Simone. 'Does that answer your question?'

'Not in the slightest,' said a disgruntled Gabrielle. 'I knew you'd be an unreliable witness. Why do you think I wanted to be there?'

A discreet knocking sounded on the door. Simone flinched, and stilled, but the knocking did not get louder or more insistent. It had to be room service knocking. The door would not open to reveal Rafael this time. She hoped. Releasing her breath slowly, Simone forced tense muscles to relax and turned towards the door.

'Allow me.' Gabrielle shot her a curious glance before heading for the door and opening it to reveal a smiling Sarah bearing a trolley laden with food, elegant crystal wine glasses and white wine on ice.

'Sarah, you're just in time,' said Gabrielle as she helped Sarah wheel the trolley into the room. 'Did you see Rafe earlier?'

'Yep.'

'How did he look?'

'Bothered.'

'What about hot?' asked Gaby the shameless.

'He always looks hot,' said Sarah, putting a hand to her heart. 'Hot and bothered was a new look for him, but frankly, he wore it well. Shall I pour wine for two?'

'Double over here,' murmured Simone.

Gabrielle snickered. 'You *do* still want him.'

'I didn't say that,' Simone said indignantly. 'Sarah, did I say that?'

Sarah dimpled and handed her a wine glass filled perilously close to overflowing. 'So you're the one.'

'Pardon?'

'The one who's got him all riled. The one who got away. The one who ruined him for all other women,' offered Sarah expansively.

'Oh, that's harsh,' said Gabrielle, accepting a much smaller glass of wine from Sarah. 'Harsh, yet disturbingly accurate.'

'I did *not* ruin him for all other women.'

'Not *knowingly*,' conceded Gabrielle. 'If you had I couldn't love you the way I do.'

'Anyway, define "ruined",' argued Simone. 'He didn't look particularly ruined to me.' He'd looked dangerously, broodingly desirable. 'I'll bet *plenty* of other women have found his attentions more than adequate.'

'I'm sure they have,' murmured Gabrielle soothingly. 'The point being that he never attends them for very *long*. More wine?'

Simone had forgotten all about the wine. She sipped, and sipped again. They were big sips. Fortifying sips. It was very good wine.

'You need a plan,' said Gabrielle.

'I have a plan. It's called stay for your wedding and then leave.'

'You need a better plan,' said Gabrielle, sipping her own wine thoughtfully. 'Sarah, can you ask Inigo if we can bring forward the menu planning to this afternoon? Say 5:00 p.m.?'

'I can,' said Sarah. 'And he will. But he won't be happy about it.'

'Tell him there's a bottle of Angels Tears in it for him. That ought to cheer him up.'

'It'd cheer me up,' said Sarah as she headed for the door.

'Who's Inigo?' asked Simone.

'The restaurant manager,' murmured Gabrielle. 'He's very fussy about food choice. Anyone would think he was French.'

'Most of us just think he's mad,' said Sarah from the door. 'But he does run a fine restaurant service. He's been trying to nail Gabrielle down to a meal plan for the reception for weeks.'

'I was waiting for you to arrive,' said Gabrielle to Simone as Sarah closed the door behind her on her way out. 'My decision-making powers have temporarily deserted me. Mind you, if you prefer one thing and I prefer another we'll still be without a decision. I'd better call Rafe. He can meet us there.' She offered up an encouraging smile. 'You don't mind if he joins us, do you?'

'I don't mind,' said Simone carefully. 'But Rafael might not be enamoured of the notion.'

'He doesn't have to be enamoured,' replied Gabrielle blithely as she fished her mobile from her handbag. 'Although I'm not ruling it out.' She pressed a couple of buttons and put the phone to her ear. 'He just has to be there.'

Which was how, at exactly five past five that afternoon, Simone came to be examining plateware patterns in a sumptuously appointed private dining room with Gabrielle the indecisive and Inigo the sorely put upon. Rafael had not yet arrived, but the spectre of him doing so made concentrating difficult.

'What about the pink and ivory Limoges design?' asked Gabrielle.

'Very elegant,' murmured Simone.

'Or just the plain white Limoges with the silver trim,' said Inigo, pointing to it in the cabinet. 'Food sits well on that plate too.'

'Safe choice,' agreed Simone.

'Not helping,' said Gabrielle.

Simone sighed. 'Inigo, do you mind if we take some plates from the cabinet and set a few table places for comparison? We'll need silverware, napkins and glassware as well.'

Inigo did not mind. Inigo was all for a decision. Any decision. He opened half a dozen sideboard drawers and indicated the silverware choices. Opened sideboard cupboards to reveal the glassware.

'Is the restaurant décor similar to this?' Simone gestured around the antique-filled room with its dark wooden floors and tables and fireplace filled with fresh flowers. Inigo assured her it was. Simone glanced at Gabrielle next. Gabrielle looked overwhelmed. 'You've seen all this before?'

Gabrielle nodded. 'As far as I'm concerned it's *all* beautiful.'

Yes, it was. Fortunately, some of it was more beautiful than the rest. 'And you really want my input? You do realise that the only opinion that counts in all of this is yours?'

'I do,' said Gabrielle. 'And I have no idea what I want. Apart from Lucien beside me on my wedding day. The rest could be sawdust.'

'Yes, well, it *could* be,' murmured Simone, grinning at Inigo's aghast expression. 'But spare a thought for the rest of us.' Simone stood and surveyed the tableware on offer. 'Inigo, we'll need the Swarovski glassware—no, not the large red wine glass, the medium-sized one, and the glasses for the white wine and the champagne too, *merci*. Then the silverware with the cutaway groove. Yes, please. Then the pink and ivory plates, the café-au-lait coloured napkins and we'll finish with the pewter hedgehog napkin rings for whimsy.' She surveyed the flowers in the fireplace with an eye to colour and form and finally plucked half a dozen old roses in creams, palest pink, and apricot and placed them above the setting.

'What about tablecloths?' asked Inigo.

'No tablecloths on this woodgrain,' murmured Simone, sliding her hand along the gleaming woodwork. 'Let's set another place. This time I'd like the white Hermès plates with the red and gold swirl, and to go with them the plain-edged silverware and white napkins.'

'*Very* nice,' said Inigo as the second place setting took shape with gratifying speed. 'What else?' Inigo held up a crystal champagne flute with a fine gold swirl running through it, and at Simone's nod added it to the setting along with plainer wine glasses for the red and white wine. Simone chose another handful of the old roses from the basket in the fireplace, bolder hues this time, and added them to the table. Finally, she stood back and surveyed the two settings critically.

'The Hermès gets my vote,' she murmured, for it was gorgeous and vibrant and the room could take it. 'Gaby? What do you think?'

'This better not be your emergency, Gabrielle.'

Dark-edged, softly spoken words, threaded through with impatience. Simone felt the slide of them across her body as if a whip had lashed lightly across the skin on her back. Not to inflict pain, not yet, but the threat was there, and with that threat came the deeper knowledge that there was pleasure to be had in pain and that Rafael was more than capable of helping her find it.

Her pulse would triple, her heart would ache, and her eyes would be greedy once she'd turned to face him, and there wasn't a thing she could do about it.

She took her time turning to face him, knowing as she did so that she would find no welcome in his eyes. Knowing too that she would force him to acknowledge her and that she would pay for her boldness with pleasure and with pain. Oh, yes. There was a sweet, aching pleasure to be taken here and take it she would.

'*Bonjour*, Rafael.' He was still wearing his work clothes. He still looked dangerously out of sorts. Her heartbeat thudded its approval. 'Big day in the field?'

'Evening, princess,' he murmured, those brilliant blue eyes shaded with no small measure of mockery. 'This your idea?'

'Mine? No.' Simone waved a hand in Gabrielle's direction. Gabrielle waved languidly back, amusement writ plain across her features. 'I'm just trying to be a good bridesmaid and get through the day as best I can. But seeing you're here, pick a place setting, any setting. As long as it's one of the two on the table.'

Rafael surveyed the table settings, but not for long. 'The one with the red.'

'Decisive,' murmured Gabrielle.

'Isn't he?' agreed Simone, never mind that his opinion echoed hers.

'Isn't that what you want?' said Rafael.

'It's what I want,' said Inigo with a flirtatious leer in Rafe's direction.

The look Rafael sent the maître d' was darkly amused. 'Inigo, you know I don't play ball.'

'Oh, I *know*.' Inigo's smile came swift and un-daunted. 'It's just so *hard* to find that kind of authori-tarian streak amongst the ladies.'

'Give him time,' Gabrielle murmured to Simone. 'He's only just seen you. He'll figure it out.'

'Well, while he does, tell me which table setting you prefer,' said Simone. 'The red is the bolder choice of the two, but then, you're not exactly a wallflower. You probably don't need reminding that neither is Luc.'

Gabrielle's smile was that of a satisfied woman. 'The red *is* gorgeous.'

'Inigo, if I can interrupt the courtship process for a moment, we have a decision on the table décor,' Simone said smoothly, and had the satisfaction of seeing Rafe's eyes narrow in silent warning. She acknowledged his warning with the tilt of her lips. She'd seen many a woman flirt with Rafael over the years. She'd never seen a man attempt to until now. It was enough to make a woman start humming a little YMCA ditty to help set the mood.

'Ooh, my favourite song,' declared Inigo.

'Mine *too*,' she said.

'Stay,' she heard Gabrielle mutter from somewhere to her left.

'So help me, Gabrielle, you'll owe me for this,' came Rafe's muttered reply and Simone's smile widened.

'Will a thousand thank-yous be sufficient payment?'

'No.'

'I'll clean your house,' whispered Gabrielle next. 'Twice.'

'Who cares?'

'Please, Rafael.'

The please was the clincher. When Rafael loved, it was all or nothing. It was his greatest weakness or his most beloved strength and Simone knew before he spoke that he would have no defence against Gabrielle's pleading.

'What do you need?' he said gruffly.

'You. Here,' said Gabrielle.

The quietly spoken words echoed Simone's deepest yearnings. The humming stopped. 'Inigo, we'll use the setting on the left,' she said with a tired smile and tried to quell the desire to reach out and capture some of Rafe's tenderness for herself. She wouldn't know what to do with it if he gave it, and that was God's truth. 'What's next?'

'The menu,' said Inigo, effortlessly following her train of thought, which was no mean feat all things considered. 'Unless you'd rather start with the table wine choices and work back to the menu from there? I won't tell the chef if you don't.'

'At the risk of sounding decisive, I'm all for choosing the wine first,' said Simone. 'Gaby?'

'All we need is some still white wine for the tables,' said Gabrielle as Inigo placed a leather-bound folder on the table in front of her. 'We have the cabernet sauvignon and the champagne sorted.'

'We certainly do,' said Inigo. 'The chef keeps sneaking into the cool room to look at the champagne and genuflect. Would you like a tasting bottle brought up?'

'Yes,' said Simone and Gabrielle in unison, never mind the half-empty bottle of white wine back in Simone's room.

'And for the red I've set aside the Angels Tears,' continued Inigo as he headed for the doorway. 'I'll bring a bottle of that up for you too.'

'I thought your wine was called Angels Landing,' said Simone, harking back to an earlier thought.

'Most of it is,' said Gabrielle. 'This is private stock. Rafe and I bottled it years ago, just after I arrived on his doorstep. He let me name it.'

'That's quite a name.' Simone sought Rafael's gaze. He stared back at her impassively, as if determined to give her nothing to work with. No words. No emotion. Nothing. Surely, he could give her *something* to work with. It didn't have to be tenderness. Civility would do.

'It's possible I may have been a little morose at the time,' confessed Gabrielle. 'What can I say? I was sweet sixteen and I'd just been kissed. I'd also just been banished to what felt a lot like the end of the earth. It wasn't one of my better years, but it had its blessings,' she added, with a quiet smile in Rafe's direction. 'The wine is good,' she said, turning her attention back to Simone. 'It's very good.'

Simone believed her. 'I look forward to tasting it. Meanwhile, shall we take a look at the table whites they have on offer?' Ignoring Rafe, she tried to get on with the task at hand. What had Gabrielle chosen to go with the finger food earlier? 'A Semillon Blanc?'

Gabrielle nodded and flipped the pages over until she reached the required section. Simone perused the list over Gabrielle's shoulder. It was a big list. Most of the wines were Australian. She knew nothing of Australian white wines. 'Something regional?'

'Not this region,' said Rafael, finally offering input. 'Red wine rules here, not white. And if it has to complement the Caverness, I suggest you start at the bottom of the list and stay there. This one.' He pointed to one of the labels. 'Or these two.'

'Decisiveness *is* quite appealing in a man at times, isn't it?' murmured Gabrielle.

'Oh, quite,' agreed Simone, while her gaze clashed with Rafael's in a battle that had nothing to do with the

words and everything to do with establishing which of
them was better at controlling the raw and powerful
need that ran between them. 'Such a pity Inigo isn't
here to witness it. We could have watched him swoon.'

'You can watch me swoon instead,' said Gabrielle.
'I've just found the rack price for those wines.' She
looked to her brother. 'I can't ask Harrison to pay that
price for wine.'

Harrison was Rafael and Gabrielle's father, remembered Simone. Josien had refused him access to his
children in their younger years, but Rafe had gone to
him when he'd left Caverness. Harrison had welcomed
him. He'd welcomed Gabrielle too, when she'd been
unceremoniously bundled off to Australia. A generous
man, thought Simone. And a patient one. What was it
that he farmed again? Some sort of beef cattle. Lots of
ups and downs in the beef-cattle market. 'Ask Luc to
pay for the wine,' she suggested.

'Ask *me*,' said Rafael with a lopsided smile that
tugged at Simone's heart. 'How many times are you
planning on getting married, angel?'

'Once,' said Gabrielle with quiet conviction.

'Then do it right,' he said gently. 'Harrison will pay.
Try stopping him. And so will I.' He spared a lightning
glance for Simone. 'We don't need Duvalier money.'

'Isn't pride a sin?' murmured Simone, goaded into
retaliation. 'I thought it was.'

'Stick around,' he said grimly. 'I'll give you a taste
of all seven.'

'If you say so.' Simone allowed herself a brief fantasy interlude. Rafael's mouth on hers, hot and devour-
ing. Her hands on him, desperate and racing. Desire bit
deep and flared beneath her skin, overwhelming
caution and reason and straining her control. How far

could she stretch his seemingly iron control? 'Can lust be next?'

'Oh, boy,' muttered Gabrielle. 'Just pretend I'm not here. Come to think of it, I've just remembered a very important meeting I should be at.'

'Stay,' said Simone and Rafael in unison.

'This was your idea, remember?' added Simone.

'What the *hell* was I thinking?' said Gabrielle. 'Oh, yeah. I remember now. I was trying to help the two of you arrive at some sort of truce before my *wedding*. Silly me.'

Simone felt a stab of contrition. It joined the lust and mingled surprisingly well. Probably the latent Catholic in her. 'I'm sorry, dear heart. I will behave.'

Inigo reappeared, bearing champagne in an ice bucket in one hand and a bottle of red wine in the other. 'Do I hear the satisfied silence that comes of having made a swift decision?' he asked hopefully as he set the wines on the table.

'Not quite,' said Gabrielle. 'But we've narrowed it down to three.'

'Which ones?'

Gabrielle told him.

Inigo beamed. Inigo preened. 'You won't be disappointed. Mind you, the thought of how long it's going to take you to pick a favourite from that selection fills me with terror,' he said, presenting the champagne to Simone for approval, and, at her nod, popping the cork and deftly filling three glasses in rapid succession.

'Take the rest of the bottle through to the kitchen, please, Inigo,' said Simone. 'Tell the chef it's his for the tasting and that we'd like his thoughts on what sort of canapés he thinks might best accompany it.'

'Are you serious?' Inigo glanced towards Rafael as if for confirmation. 'Is she serious?'

Rafael nodded. 'She likes to delegate from on high.'

'Well, that's one interpretation,' said Simone sweetly. How could she be expected to behave in the face of Rafael's constant baiting? 'I like to think of it as letting the experts do their job.' She picked up the ice bucket and handed it to Inigo. 'Kitchen,' she said.

'Kitchen,' murmured Inigo. 'I'm on my way. I'm seeing the princess's master plan unfold and I'm loving it. I'll just pour a glass for myself as well as one for the chef and wax lyrical over the bouquet for a moment or two before suggesting that we call his apprentice and my offsider in to work tonight so that we can concentrate more fully on the weighty issue of planning a menu around such wines. Then I'll go and get the whites you requested. Right after I uncork the red for you.' Which he did. 'There we go. Breathe, little cry baby, breathe. I have a hunch I'll be seeing *you* later.' Humming cheerfully, Inigo made his exit.

'Congratulations,' murmured Rafael. 'You've made a conquest.'

'Haven't we all,' countered Simone with the tilt of an eyebrow.

'Simone,' said Gabrielle sternly, 'don't tease. I can't be held responsible for the consequences if you do. Rafe's not twelve any more. He's unlikely to put a frog in your shoe in reply.'

'Pity,' said Simone with wistful sigh. 'I like frogs.' As a child she'd built homes for them in the shady nooks in the gardens of Caverness, and Rafael knew it. The frogs he'd put in her shoes had been gifts for her, not retaliation for her teasing, and *she* knew it. 'To frogs,' she said, and reached for the champagne.

'To the children of Caverness,' said Gabrielle, picking up another glass of the gently bubbling liquid. 'May they never weep again.'

'Lovely,' said Simone approvingly. 'Although possibly a little optimistic.'

'Just how much wine have you two already had?' asked Rafael.

'He had to go and spoil it,' said Gabrielle, eyeing her brother darkly.

'No sense of occasion at all,' agreed Simone, sipping her champagne. 'Oh, this is *good*. Rafael, try some.' She wasn't inebriated. She didn't think for one minute that a glass of champagne, even if it was a superb vintage, would change Rafael's opinion of her. She just wanted Rafe to be able to relax around her, just a little, so that she could relax, so that maybe, just maybe, they could get through this evening without bloodshed.

Rafael's lips tightened as he reached for the only glass of champagne still left on the table. Half of it went in one long swallow. The man was obviously thirsty and royally out of sorts. Maybe she'd been a bit hasty in sending the rest of the bottle to the kitchen.

'It's Luc's favourite vintage,' she told him. 'Do you like it?'

'It's superb,' he said curtly. 'Not that you need my opinion.'

'Just checking,' she said. 'I do that a lot. Occupational hazard.'

'And what exactly is it that you do these days, princess? Besides delegate, that is.'

Ooh, he was asking for trouble. She didn't care how big and beautiful he was. 'Oh, nothing much,' she said airily. 'I spend a bit of time pottering around the gardens of Caverness. I oversee the running and maintenance of the chateau. I run the European marketing arm of the Duvalier winemaking dynasty. That sort of thing.'

'Don't forget all the hiring and firing,' injected Gabrielle. 'You do that too.'

Simone shook her head. 'Luc usually does all that.'

'But you were the one to suggest that Josien find work elsewhere,' said Gabrielle quietly.

'Oh.' She took a deep breath. 'That. So I was.'

Rafael's sudden stillness unnerved her. The intensity of his gaze unnerved her more.

'You fired Josien?' Rafe's voice was mild. Too mild. *'You?'*

'Yes.' Simone tried hard not to quail beneath the onslaught of that searching blue gaze. She'd fired his mother from a position Josien had held for almost thirty years, but not without good reason. Rafe hadn't been there. He hadn't seen for himself how untenable Gabrielle's position as Luc's wife would have been had Josien stayed in residence as housekeeper to Caverness. 'Me.'

'Why?'

Now *there* was a question in need of a careful answer. Never mind that Rafe had been baiting her and she him ever since he'd stepped into the room. Never mind that he'd been estranged from Josien for years. Criticising a man's mother was never a sensible thing to do. 'Because I wanted her gone from Caverness.'

'Why?'

'Can we please not have this conversation?' she said.

'Too late,' he said. 'We're already having it. Why did you fire Josien?'

'Because it was time she left Caverness,' she said curtly, and cursed him for pushing her for answers she didn't want to give. 'Because I refused to sit back and watch her poison the happiness Gabrielle and Luc had found.' She lifted her chin. 'Because I could.'

Rafael drained the rest of his champagne. He looked as if he were swallowing the bitterest of pills rather than vintage champagne. 'Good,' he said gruffly.

'Pardon?' squeaked Simone.

'I'd have done the same,' he said.

He… *'What?'*

'You heard.'

'Well, yes, but…' Had he really just given his *approval*? 'Was that a compliment?'

'I don't know,' he said with a twist of his lips. 'It could have been. It was hellishly hard to say aloud.'

'I think it might have been,' she said, and with a swift and challenging smile, 'Does this mean we're friends?'

'No, it means we have a common foe and I'm impressed by your ruthlessness.'

Was that the shadow of a smile in his eyes? Hard to tell, but she thought it might be. 'I had a good teacher,' she said with a shrug. 'He taught me how to protect the people I love. I was a little slow on the uptake, but I got there eventually.'

'Josien's not coming to the wedding, by the way,' said Gabrielle with a lightness that didn't quite mask her disappointment. 'She says she's not yet recovered enough from her pneumonia to attempt the travel.'

'But surely you expected as much?' said Simone. 'I thought you held the wedding here so as to keep her *away*?'

'Well, yes, that *was* one of the reasons for holding it here,' acknowledged Gabrielle. 'But not the only one. I'm having second thoughts.'

'Don't,' said Rafael, and the hardness was back in

his eyes. He loved hard, did Rafael. Simone didn't need to be reminded that he hated hard too.

'Maybe you'll pay her a quick visit on the way back from your honeymoon,' said Simone gently. 'Maybe given time and happiness of her own she'll come to accept who and what you are.'

'Didn't the person who showed you how to protect the ones you love teach you not to believe in fairy tales?' murmured Rafael.

'Yes, but it never stuck,' said Simone. 'Unlike him, I believe in forgiveness and redemption. I believe that with a little effort from both parties, a failed relationship can be rebuilt. Maybe not to what people *hope* for, but something. Something worthwhile.'

'Optimist,' he said.

'Coward.'

'Oh, boy,' said Gabrielle as the maître d' bustled back into the room.

'More wine,' said Inigo cheerfully. 'Lots and lots of wine.' He glanced at Rafael's empty champagne flute. 'Who's a thirsty boy, then?' And in a whispered undertone to Simone, 'The chef wishes to propose to you. When's a good time?'

'Maybe later,' said Simone as Inigo opened the three white wines and organised glassware.

'I'd stay,' said Inigo flashing her a wide white smile, 'but I know you need no guidance when it comes to tasting wine and I have to return to the kitchen and guard my champagne.' He pointed towards a little brass bell on the sideboard. 'Tinkle when you're done.'

'I'll come with you,' said Gabrielle hurriedly. 'I need to have a word with the chef about a duck dish for the menu.'

'And here I thought your decision-making abilities had deserted you,' said Simone dryly.

'They're back,' said Gabrielle emphatically. 'But feel free to choose a white wine in my absence. Just don't...' she seemed at a loss for words '...fight, okay? Play nice.' Shooting her brother a dark glare, Gabrielle followed Inigo from the room.

Silence followed their departure, and hot on the heels of that silence came the prickling awareness that she was alone with a man she'd once lost her heart to, and that most of her bravado had left the room with Gabrielle.

'Shall we attempt conversation?' she said, finally meeting his fathomless blue gaze. 'Or shall we just drink?'

Wordlessly he picked up a bottle of wine and poured for them both. Good answer.

She sipped and tasted, giving the wine her utmost attention. So did Rafael.

While the silence grew.

'Too light?' she said finally.

'Yes,' he said, and poured the next.

This one had more body and a delicate fruity finish. 'Nice,' she murmured. Rafael said nothing, just moved on to the next.

They sipped. They tasted. As far as Simone was concerned, this was another very fine wine. A little more robust than the second one. A peppery low note in there somewhere. Smooth clean finish. But the second wine had her vote.

'Which one, princess?'

'I quite like it when you call me princess,' she said reflectively. 'It feels a lot like an endearment and a challenge all rolled into one.' She sipped her wine and risked a glance in his direction. 'I thought you should know.'

'Which wine?' he repeated tightly. No princesses present.

'The second one.'

He nodded and set the bottle aside. Whether he agreed with her choice was open to speculation. Maybe he simply wanted to get the wine choosing over with so he could *leave*. Maybe that wasn't such a bad idea.

He reached for the red wine and poured for them both. Angels Tears. Evocative name. Beautifully coloured wine. She sipped, and sipped again. It was divine. 'Oh, yes,' she murmured. 'Luc's going to love this.'

'And you?' Rafael had yet to touch his own glass. His eyes were on her, searching for her reaction to his wine. 'Do you like it?'

'Do you care?'

He looked away, towards the fireplace with the flowers. 'No.'

No. Heaviness descended, and with it regret for what could have been and wasn't. It didn't have to be like this. It really didn't. 'It's brilliant,' she said quietly. 'But then, so are you. You always were.'

He flinched as if she'd hit him.

Simone bowed her head and cupped her hands around her wine goblet.

'Tell Gabrielle I had to leave.' Rafe's voice sounded strained and husky, as if he'd already shouted himself hoarse. 'Tell her I'm sorry, and that everything will be okay on her wedding day.'

'I will.' She gazed at the dark and shimmering liquid in the goblet. The image blurred. More tears were coming. Her tears.

'Simone?' he said next, and she closed her eyes and let the pain of her name on his lips slice through her because with it came pleasure and take it she would.

'Rafael.'

'I'm glad you liked the wine.'

She waited until his footsteps had receded before she finally let her tears fall. 'Me too.'

CHAPTER THREE

'You do know that you're being an ass?'

Rafe looked up from the paperwork on his desk and regarded his sister through narrowed eyes with grim humour. She'd been circling around the topic of his treatment of Simone now for at least half an hour, waiting for an opening that he hadn't given her. This wasn't the tack he would have advised her to take with him, but he figured she'd find that out soon enough. 'How so?'

'The way you're making Simone feel unwelcome.'

'She is unwelcome.'

'She's my bridesmaid. She's the sister of the groom. And pretty soon she's going to be family.'

Rafe scowled. He really didn't need the reminder.

'Tell me, Rafe, what are you going to do come Christmas time when we're all together? Or when you're invited to the christening?'

'What christening?' His gaze flew to his sister's stomach. His own stomach lurched unevenly. Caverness was hard on its children. *All* of its children. He hoped to hell that with this child, things would be different. 'You're not…?'

'Not yet,' she murmured. 'But some day I plan to be, many times over, and I want you in my children's lives.'

Oh, dear Lord, now they were multiplying. 'Couldn't we have this discussion *after* you have them?'

Gabrielle eyed him sternly. 'My point is that you and Simone are two of the three most important people in my life. Can't you at least *try* to be in the same room as her for more than five minutes?'

'Five minutes is a long time,' he said. Especially when a man was torn between wanting to strip a woman down to her skin and bury himself inside her, or, conversely, strip her to her skin, tie her to a bedpost and flay her for causing him such pain. Either way, getting her naked seemed to be a priority. 'I've been working my way up from three.'

'Can't you just—?'

'No,' he interrupted, in a low, controlled voice that nonetheless carried with it a warning she would do well to heed. 'I can't.'

'Why not? Why not invite her over and show her the vineyard? She'd love to see what we've done here. I know she would. But whenever I say come over, she says no.'

'Smart woman.'

'Yes, she is. Also beautiful, generous, kind, and the only woman you've ever truly loved,' finished Gabrielle cuttingly. 'Which is why you're being an ass.'

'Isn't this where you came in?'

'Yes.' Gabrielle regarded him darkly. 'But it wouldn't have had to be a circular argument if you'd shown some sense. You told me I was stuck in the past when I said I wanted to return to France. You said I was mad to go and visit Josien. Well, maybe I *was* mad to think that Josien would want to see me, but I tried, and I've moved on, and now I'm marrying the man I love beyond measure, and Simone, my beloved childhood friend, is back in my life. I'm not the one stuck in the past, Rafael. I'm not the one who's too scared to look back because there's too much pain there that I haven't dealt with yet.' Her eyes begged his forgiveness. Her words cut him to the bone. 'You are.'

When Rafael worked, he worked hard. When Rafael brooded he worked harder. He'd taken to the fields after his words with Gabrielle. Taken the Toyota and a trailer and an axe so he could cut down a dead and dangerously leaning tree. It would drop down on a border fence regardless of where he placed his cut so he'd brought the fence cutters too, and wire and materials for rebuilding the fence later. He might get around to putting the fence back up today.

He might not.

Why the hell would someone want to look back on a childhood like his? On a mother who'd ruled with an iron rod, or a leather horsewhip or whatever else had come to hand. A mother whose moods had see-sawed faster than light. Remote one minute, a banshee the next, but never *ever* loving towards her children. Gabrielle she'd tolerated, on occasion. Her feelings for her son had been crystal clear and brutally unwavering.

She hated him.

Rafael smiled grimly. Over the years, the feeling had become entirely mutual.

The slam of his axe bit deep into the tree's heartwood. The axe was small. The tree was huge. It would take a while to bring it down.

Good.

He needed the exercise and he sure as hell needed the release. And as for being too scared to revisit his time with Simone…

Thwack went the axe into the wood. He wrenched it free and swung again. This time when it lodged into the wood he left it there. He returned to the ute, reached in the window for his phone and dialled the guest house. When Sarah answered he got her to put the call through to Simone's room.

'I'm felling a tree,' he said when she answered. 'Then I'm repairing a fence. And then I'm showing you around the vineyard. I will be filthy. I will be hard to communicate with. I will be at the Angels Landing cellar door at four.'

There was a pause. A very lengthy pause.

Then, 'I'll be there,' Simone said dryly, and hung up.

Gabrielle laughed when Simone relayed the gist of the conversation to her. She belly laughed when Simone relayed the conversation word for word.

'Stop it,' Simone ordered. 'Did I laugh at you when you were worried about seeing Luc again? No. I gave you sympathy.'

'You *have* my sympathy,' said Gabrielle earnestly, right before the laughter started up again. 'He's such an ass. Do you have a plan?'

'Working on it.' Simone settled back against the bed head. 'The only way Rafael seems to think he can deal with me is if he calls all the shots. I've been very patient with him, Gabrielle. Extremely patient. But you *do* realise it has to stop.'

'Oh, I *do*.' Gabrielle tried for solemnity, she really did. But moments later she was lying on her back on the end of the bed as mirth took hold of her again.

'Stop that.' Simone poked at her with her foot. 'I need you coherent. I need a plan.'

Gabrielle wiped at her eyes as her laughter subsided.

Eventually, she sat back up. 'Well, it's about time,' she said. 'Does it involve seduction? Puppies? Phero-mones?'

'No. That would be a threatening move on my part and his defences would go up. We don't want that.'

'No, we most certainly don't.' Gabrielle drummed her fingers on the bedspread. 'Why don't you play the damsel in distress and have him come to your rescue?'

'Because he wouldn't,' said Simone dryly. 'No, for that to work properly I'd have to legitimately *be* in distress, and I hate that role.'

Gabrielle started to grin. Simone stopped her with a glance. 'He needs to stop seeing me as a threat, but I can't be seen to be weak. He needs to see me as an ally.'

'Alliance is good,' said Gabrielle cautiously. 'Who's the common enemy?'

'There's the catch. Apart from Josien, who's not here and to my way of thinking seems to be going some way towards improving her relationship with you and losing her enemy status into the bargain, we don't have one.'

'What about a common goal?'

'Common goals are good, and I think we may have a common goal in wanting your wedding day to be a magical one. I wanted to ask you…' Simone took the time to phrase her question with care. 'Rafe doesn't have a problem with you marrying into the Duvalier family, does he?'

'No,' said Gabrielle with a quick shake of her head. 'Oh, Rafael knows as well as I do that there'll be chal-lenges ahead and that some people won't approve of this union—but he's not one of them. He knows I'm marrying the man I love, Simone. He knows Luc's heart is true. Rafe may not be entirely comfortable with gaining you for a sister-in-law, but he's given my marriage to Lucien his backing and his blessing. He may be an ass,' said Gabrielle with a grimace, 'but he's *my* ass, and he only wants what's best for me. I think you should take his invitation as a sign that he's trying to make his peace with you. Whether he *will* or not is anyone's guess. But he's trying.'

Simone put her hands to her head and rubbed hard before finally smoothing her hands over her hair. She'd had a sleepless night and a jet-lagged day and she needed a strategy for dealing with Rafael that would keep her heart safe. So far, she'd come up empty.

'He is *very* good with damsels in distress,' said Gabrielle again. 'It's that overprotective streak that was honed to perfection during the childhood he tries hard to forget. You couldn't just—'

'No,' said Simone abruptly. To call on Rafael's vulnerability—the very protectiveness that had once made her love him so deeply—and play it for a weakness?

'No, Gabrielle. I could not.'

By ten to four the tree was down, the fence was fixed and Rafe was heartily wishing that he'd brought the chainsaw along with him to finish the job. The axe was blunt, his shoulders ached, and the release that he'd sought in hard physical labour had so far eluded him. He was hot, he was bothered, and why the hell he'd let Gabrielle goad him into spending time alone with Simone was a mystery to him.

He wanted a cold shower and an even colder beer, and he wanted to forget he'd ever suggested showing Simone around the vineyard he'd brought back from ruin.

He wanted a woman, wanton and willing. One he could lose himself in for a time and walk away from unscathed.

Not Simone, sensual and fearless, who would call forth desires too deeply held.

Not Simone.

Cursing beneath his breath, he loaded up the ute and headed for the cellars. With any luck she'd be running late and he'd have time to wash down and cool off before she arrived. With a bit more luck she might have changed her mind about touring the vineyard with him altogether.

A silver-grey Audi sat in the car park beside the cellar door.

A dark-haired ingénue wearing a vivid pink strapless sundress leaned against it and watched his approach.

Guess not.

'A tree?' she said once he stood before her.

'And a fence.' He'd warned her that he would be filthy. He looked down at his T-shirt where tree sap and splinters vied for supremacy. Possibly not this filthy, but there was a tap and a sink inside and he had a spare T-shirt in the ute. He found the shirt and headed for the door. 'Come on through.'

Simone followed him into the building, a gable-roofed corrugated-iron shed of muted greens and greys. It didn't have the ancient appeal of the champagne storage caves of Caverness, but it suited the landscape well enough, and the scarred and mismatched wooden furnishings of the tasting room held a certain rustic charm.

'Let me get rid of some of this dirt before I take you through to the vats,' he said as he headed for the washbasin behind the bar.

'Of course.' So far, Rafael more than lived up to his promise of general dishevelment. He had the body for it though, long and leanly muscled, and a perfection of face guaranteed to cut through any amount of dirt. As far as Simone was concerned, the intensity of his brilliant blue gaze served only to clinch the deal. Dirt or no dirt, Rafael Alexander was a breathtakingly beautiful man.

He knew it. How could he not?

But his looks did not define him. There was more to him than that. A kindness of soul that warred with the fierceness of his emotions. A protective streak, honed razor-sharp by the circumstances of his childhood. A will to succeed that bordered on obsessive, and when he focused his attentions on something or someone… well, a woman didn't easily forget such a time.

She'd never managed to.

Simone took a seat on the customer side of the bar, fully intending to study the wine-tasting list. She might have even managed to pay attention to the vintages on offer if Rafael hadn't chosen that particular moment to peel his T-shirt from his body.

She tried to draw breath, tried to look away, but the latter was impossible and the former took determined effort. She found her breath, and then her voice. 'Your back—'

He had his back towards her. He stilled, but he didn't turn around.

'Something against tattoos?' he asked quietly.

'No.' Dear heaven, no. 'It's exquisite. But the words…'
Never look back.

He sluiced his face and arms; he took his sweet time before finally reaching for a nearby hand towel and turning to face her. 'What about them?'

'They just seem so…' How could she explain the impact of those harsh, hard words carved into his skin, no matter how beautiful the pattern they made?

'…Desolate. Surely some things are worth remembering?' A young girl and a handsome older boy coaxing a tiny frog out of her boot and into the home she'd made for it. A first kiss sweeter than sunshine. A first love's gentle caress. She sought his gaze and held it. 'Aren't they?'

He didn't answer. Just looked away, picked up his clean T-shirt and pulled it on.

'When did you get it?' she asked next. She couldn't seem to let go of the notion that he'd paid somebody to cut those words into his skin.

She didn't think he was going to answer that question either, but then a parody of a smile stole across his lips, and his gaze met hers, mocking and bitter. 'When I first came to Australia. Right after I left you.'

'Hmm,' she said finally, while deep down inside resentment began to build in response to the implication that his hurt, and the tattoo that went with it, were all her fault. 'I just wept for six months, cursed you for six more, and kept my happy memories of you close. I still keep them close. It must be a gender thing.'

'Maybe it's a strength of feeling thing.'

'Don't count on it,' she said tightly. How dared he turn his memory of her love for him into something weak and fleeting? How dared he paint her the villain? 'You want to forget the past, Rafael? Fine. Go ahead. It's your loss.' Anger fuelled her feet as she stalked towards him. 'You want to live for the present and look to the future? Fine. Here we are. Show me your bloody vineyard!'

'Careful, Simone.' His eyes had narrowed. A muscle worked in his jaw. 'Swearing doesn't become a lady.'

'If you had any kind of memory left you'd remember that I often take exquisite pleasure in *not* behaving like a lady. Would you like a demonstration?'

'What are you going to do, princess?' They were toe to toe. Tension radiated from him in waves. 'Hit me?'

'Oh, no.' Tempting as it was. 'You got enough of that throughout your childhood, remember? Then again, you probably don't. No, I was thinking of something a whole lot more subtle, by way of a demonstration.' She put her hand to his chest, to his heart, before finally curving it round the back of his neck and pressing her lips to the strong curve of his jaw. Gently.

'You think I didn't love you,' she murmured. Another kiss for that stubborn jaw, followed by the slow slide of her lips across to the edge of his mouth. 'You think your feelings were the stronger and that you were the only one who was left desolate and grieving.'

She gave him time to move away, she did give him that.

His chest heaved and he drew a ragged breath. But he stayed right where he was.

'You're wrong,' she whispered, and set her lips to his. Lord have mercy on her soul.

His lips were warm and firm. And closed. She touched the tip of her tongue to the crease in them and tasted salt. She felt the shudder that ripped through him, but his mouth stayed stubbornly closed to her. She started to pull away. Experiment over. Experiment failed.

And then his hand came up to cup her face, his lips opened beneath hers, a dam broke somewhere, and the world around her simply disappeared.

Reckless. She was so damned reckless. She always had been, especially when it came to making love. Rafe deepened the kiss, revelling in her abandoned response. The way her fingers curled into his hair, the way that greedy, generous mouth felt against his. Memories crashed down on him. He remembered that mouth, remembered marking her body with his mouth. He'd never forgotten.

Desire ate at him and she let him feed, encouraging his possession while her scent wrapped around him and clouded his thinking.

And then he closed his hands around her waist and dragged her against him as she wound her arms around his neck and all rational thought stopped. There was only heat and need, such a fierce and roiling need.

Simone's lips clinging to his, her body so soft against his hardness, and an ache that wouldn't be eased until he was buried inside her. His body burned for more. The ragged stitching holding his heart together threatened to unravel as he took and tasted as if it were his last drink before hell.

'Remember me,' she whispered. 'Remember this.'

He heard the words. And the wound on his heart tore wide open.

He cursed savagely and dragged himself free of her. Of memories he didn't want. Of a kiss he couldn't handle. He cursed again and turned away. One step, and then another while he fought to master the desire that rode him and attempted to recover some of his sanity.

Back to the sink to fill his hands with rushing cold water from the tap so he could splash it on his face and his hair. His T-shirt stayed on. Old pain remained hidden but she knew it was there now and he cursed her for that insight. She should never have come here. She should have known to let sleeping beasts lie.

He reached for the towel and buried his face in it, before tossing it to the bench and turning to face her.

She looked shattered. Dishevelled. And beaten. Not

at all the calmly composed mistress of the Duvalier champagne empire.

'That really wasn't a good idea, was it?' she said shakily.

'No.'

No, thought Simone bleakly.

'Dammit, Simone,' he said next, and his voice was tight and hard. 'What the hell do you want from me? You asked for friendship, conditional or otherwise, and I'm doing my damnedest to deliver, but that wasn't friendship! It was *war*.'

She knew it. She wished she'd never kissed him. She wished she'd never come. 'You *wanted* war, soldier boy. From the moment you stepped from your truck,' she said defiantly. 'All I did was oblige you.'

'I did *not* want war,' he said bleakly. 'I wanted… something else. God knows what exactly, but something that would satisfy Gabrielle and the children.'

Children? Bewilderment took the edge off her defiance and her shame, and she grabbed it for the lifeline it was. 'What children?'

'Gabrielle's children.'

'Gabrielle's *pregnant*?'

'No.'

She hadn't been drinking. Swear to God, she hadn't touched a drop. But she couldn't for the life of her follow this conversation. 'Do you think that some day we might manage a simple comprehensible conversation?'

'Working on it, princess.'

'Oh, I can tell.'

'Stop,' he said curtly. 'I'm working on it. It would help a great deal if you worked on it too. Do you *want* us to be at loggerheads on Gabrielle and Luc's wedding day?'

'*No*, but—'

'Zip.' His hand signal repeated the order. 'Neither do I. We're starting again. Here and now. Do you still want to see the vineyard?'

'Yes. But not if—'

'Stop!' he ordered, exasperation writ clearly on his features. 'I swear you've become irritatingly argumentative in your old age.'

Old *age*? She was twenty-six. 'Better that than an autocratic bore.'

He sent her a sinner's smile. 'You're not bored.'

'This is never going to work,' she muttered as her body responded lovingly to that smile.

'I knew you'd see it my way eventually,' he said. 'But for the sake of this wedding, let's pretend there's at least an outside chance that it might. Twenty minutes to tour the plant. Another twenty to show you the vines, after which I'll take you up the hill and show you the view. An hour, at most, and during that time we shall attempt to find new common ground. How hard can it be?'

'You're right. We need to think positive,' said Simone. 'No touching. No talk of the past. No incendiary comments. No problem.' *She* needed to stop thinking about that heart-wrenchingly beautiful tattoo. 'Got any alcohol?'

'Follow me.'

He showed her the crushing plant, the mixing, processing, and ageing vats—stainless steel and state-of-the-art, all of them. The bottling equipment was older and labour-intensive, but his volumes were small at the moment too. Doubtless he would trade up and it would be replaced when volumes grew.

The brand-new wine storage shed stood behind the processing one and if it lacked a little something by way of character when compared with the storage caves of Caverness, well, that was only to be expected. Temperature controlled and ruthlessly organised, his oak barrels stood in neat rows, pale as sand and also very new.

He noticed her frown and gave a Gallic shrug. Seasoned oak wine barrels were a rarity in Australia and the people who had them held them, he told her. They were impossible to import. He'd had to buy new.

He kept strictly to the topic of winemaking.

Simone aided his endeavour by asking technical questions.

Rafael gave technical answers and stayed at least three metres away from her at all times.

Apart from the hungry snake of desire in the pit of her stomach, her greedy eyes, and his warning glares, everything seemed to be going very well.

Only forty-nine and a half minutes to go.

They headed for Rafe's work vehicle, a high-wheeled table-top truck and completely incompatible with a knee-baring sundress. Her dress rode up to high thigh as she settled into the passenger seat. *Damn* Gabrielle and her wardrobe suggestions. She *knew* she never should have listened to them. Rafael's hands went to the steering wheel and stayed there. His knuckles turned white. His gaze turned black.

'Fix it,' he said tightly.

She fixed it.

Rafe drove. He wasn't three metres away from her now. Simone battled the tension that came with enforced proximity and tried to think of questions that would make it go away and stay away, but she was running out of questions and Rafe's answers were getting shorter. Yes, the trellising was his design. He'd wanted maximum sunlight, better air flow through the canopy and easier picking. Yes, the companion planting worked to keep pests away. The predatory ladybirds he released onto the vines also worked to keep pest numbers low.

Yes, he did eventually have to spray towards the end of the growing season. Yes, it wiped out his ladybirds. He released new ones straight after harvest.

Yes, the ducks were in residence in order to keep the grubs down.

No, they did not have names.

He showed her the dam and the wetlands below the vines. Half a dozen waterfowl and a pair of magnificent black swans had made the wetlands their home.

The swans didn't have names either.

He drove up a steep dirt track to the top of a hill and showed her the lay of his land while the minutes ticked away, the silences grew longer, and the tension between them reached excruciatingly lofty heights.

'What time is it?' she said.

'Four thirty-eight.'

Thirty-eight minutes in each other's company without bloodshed was good. 'You about ready to call it an hour?'

'God, yes,' he muttered gruffly, and that was that.

He stood staring at the view while she got in the truck and smoothed her skirt down her legs as far as it would go. 'It's all good,' she said. 'You can get in now,' she added, and sent him a bright and guileless smile to deflect the glittering gaze he shot at her.

He got in. They started down the dirt track at speed. Rafe was clearly in a hurry to put an end to this tour. It wasn't wimpish to cling to the door handle and start reciting the Lord's Prayer, was it?

He shot her a glance, still glittering but this time tinged with amusement. He slowed down a fraction.

'I got a letter today,' he said.

Letters were good. Of course…it all depended what was in them. She eyeballed him cautiously.

'It was from someone calling himself Etienne de Morsay. Apparently, he's the head of some remote kingdom on the edge of the Pyrenees. Do you know of him?'

'Yes.' It was a startling enough statement and question to get her attention and chase pesky things like unwanted desire for dark angels bearing grudges into the shadows for a time. 'He was one of my father's school friends. We used to stay at his estate whenever my father took us to Spain. He was always very nice to Luc and me.'

Simone frowned, remembering the tightness in Luc's expression upon seeing Etienne de Morsay at the Hammerschmidt auction. 'He was also the one who bid against Luc for the Hammerschmidt vineyard. The one who pushed the price through the roof. What did he want?'

'He wants me to work for him for three months and oversee the restoration of a vineyard on his estate. He's done his homework. He knows a lot about what I've done here. I'm trying to figure out how he even knows about me.'

'Not from me.' Simone shook her head. 'I haven't had any real contact with Etienne in years. He came to Daddy's funeral. He attended the Hammerschmidt auction. Luc spoke with him afterwards.' From a distance they'd looked like jaguar and lion at war over the same prey. Gabrielle had been with them for a time, remembered Simone, but she'd cut out fast. 'Maybe Luc mentioned you. Or maybe my father did, years ago. I don't know how you turned up on his radar. What I do know is that this isn't a small commission. It's a very prestigious one with significant nonmonetary benefits attached. Etienne de Morsay is a very influential man. Restore his vineyard to glory and your reputation throughout Europe as a premiere vigneron will be assured.'

Rafael drummed his fingers on the steering wheel at her words. He said nothing for a while, just concentrated on the road ahead, and then finally he spoke again. 'De Morsay says he's in Sydney. He wants a meeting. And he wants to see the vineyard.'

'It's up to you, of course,' she said delicately, not quite sure whether Rafael was asking for her advice or making a statement. 'But I would be inclined to arrange that meeting.'

'I will.' Rafael slid her a sideways glance. 'What's it like, this little kingdom of his on the edge of the mountains?'

'Maracey?' said Simone. 'It's very rugged. A little bit wild.'

'What's its main industry? Its main source of income?'

'Not grapes,' said Simone. 'Brokerage, I think. Maracey territory is neutral ground. A lot of unofficial politicking takes place there. Daddy once said that without de Morsay diplomacy, mainstream Europe would have given up on Spain decades ago.'

They'd made it back to the cellar door car park. Rafe slid his truck into place beside the hired Audi.

'Thank you for the tour,' she said politely.

'Thank you for the information.'

They were being civil. He was not looking at her as if he wanted to bed her, strangle her or both. Clearly, it was time to leave.

'So…I'll see you at the wedding,' she said as she got out of his truck and prepared to shut the door.

'Looking forward to it,' he said.

Liar. She didn't say it aloud. Apparently she didn't have to. The look Rafe sent her acknowledged how hard he was going to find playing groomsman to her bridesmaid.

'Play your part, Simone, and I'll play mine,' he muttered. 'That's all I'm asking.'

'Of course,' she said with a bright smile that masked every last one of her tumultuous feelings towards this man, not the least being anger at his assumption that she needed to be told how to behave. 'I'm all for a wedding-day truce. On one condition.'

His vivid blue gaze hardened. 'I don't do conditions.'

He'd do this one. Simone smiled again. 'I'll keep my peace with you during this wedding ceremony and reception, Rafael. I'll do it willingly, and not for you. But afterwards…don't expect my patience with your boorish behaviour to continue.'

He smiled tightly. 'You're not bored.'

She could be gentle with him, just this once. 'Neither are you. Why is that, do you think?'

'Shut the door, Simone.'

'In a minute.' There was something else he needed to know. Something he would already know, damn him, if only he'd let himself remember the past. 'Gabrielle and Luc are wonderful together, Rafe. I want their wedding day to be perfect. I want their marriage to be a success. The demands of the Duvalier empire can be harsh and unforgiving but Luc and I are aware of that. We'll see to it that those demands don't crash down on Gabrielle all at once. We'll take good care of her. On my life and Luc's, we'll protect her as you have.'

He nodded and looked away, his jaw set. 'I know you will.'

She stepped back and slammed the passenger door shut. She didn't bother raising her hand as he drove away.

He didn't look back.

CHAPTER FOUR

GABRIELLE'S dinner fork clattered to her plate, lightly steamed carrot and snow pea still attached, as she stared at Rafael as if he'd grown horns and a tail.

'Etienne de Morsay's coming here?' she said on a rising note of panic.

'Yes. Tomorrow.' Rafe studied his sister curiously from the opposite side of the dining table. 'Is that a problem?'

'Yes,' she said tightly. 'What does he want?'

'He wants to look around the vineyard, and then he wants to discuss a vineyard restoration project he'd like me to oversee.'

'Rafe, please…' Gabrielle looked almost frightened. 'You don't want to work for this man. Cancel the meeting. Tell him he can't come. Tell him you've too many wedding preparations to attend to!'

'Everything's done. Besides, apparently he's a king. Can you cancel an audience with a king?'

'You can do any damn thing you want,' said Gabrielle fiercely. 'You owe him *nothing*.'

'Except an explanation,' said Rafael dryly. 'I'd like one too. What's going on, Gabrielle? What do you have against me conducting business with this man?'

'Nothing,' she said quickly, as if only just realising

how much her reaction would intrigue him. 'Nothing, except that I've met the man, I don't like him and I don't think we should have anything to do with him.' Gabrielle's mouth set into a stubborn line. 'He's not an honest man.'

'How so?'

'Rafe, please!' Gabrielle picked up her fork and Rafe watched in silence as her hand shook so badly that she had to put the fork back down. Bowing her head, she hid her trembling hand from his view. 'I don't want to go into it. Just…tell him not to come. It's not a good time. The wedding's in three days, Luc won't be here for another two, and I just can't cope with the thought of Etienne de Morsay right now. I can't.' Ashen-faced, she stared at him. *'Please!'*

'All right. I'll put him off until after the wedding. But then you're going to tell me what this is all about.'

Gabrielle looked away, but not before Rafael had seen in her eyes a mixture of unbearable pain, stark fear, and defiance. Rafe knew that look. He'd seen it throughout their miserable childhood, in his own eyes, as well as in Gabrielle's. He never thought he'd see it here. 'Tell me what's wrong,' he said in the dialect of their youth, in the language of Caverness and all that went with it. 'Tell me what's wrong and I'll fix it.'

'But you can't fix it.' Gabrielle stood and placed her napkin on the table. 'Not this time. No one can. Don't let him come here, Rafael. I'm begging you.'

'Shh.' Dinner forgotten, he rose and enfolded his sister in his arms as he attempted to ease her distress. 'Shh. It's all right. I won't let him come here. Just tell me why?'

'I can't.' Her arms tightened around him and she sobbed as if her heart were breaking. 'I can't.'

* * *

The day of the wedding dawned silvery and clear and Simone thanked heaven for it as she eased the curtains from the sliding door and let the peace of early morning soothe her and chase away the remnants of her troubled sleep. Gabrielle had grown increasingly withdrawn and edgy in the days leading up to the wedding and nothing Simone had done had seemed to calm her down. It hadn't been until Luc had arrived yesterday that Gabrielle had settled and regular bridal jitters had resumed. Simone could cope with the likes of those. What she didn't like was knowing that something was wrong and not knowing what, and not being able to fix it.

She hated that.

Almost as much as she hated knowing that Rafael had once again been deliberately avoiding her these past few days and that her nerves were stretched almost as thin as Gabrielle's because of it. Didn't he know that familiarity bred contempt and that absence only made the want grow stronger?

Didn't he know that seeing his hand in the wedding preparations all around her and not once seeing *him* was likely to drive her loopy? The tens of dozens of old roses that Inigo had taken delivery of yesterday and hidden in one of the cool rooms had been Rafael's doing, Inigo had told her. As was the horse-drawn carriage that would take Simone and the blushing bride from the guest house to the lakeside gazebo where the ceremony would take place.

Didn't Rafe know that a sit-down meal last night with just the four of them—Luc, Gaby, Rafe and her— would have done far more to ensure a smooth wedding day than Rafe spiriting Luc away to the vineyard last night and leaving her and Gabrielle to occupy guest-house rooms as per tradition? At least Luc and Gabrielle had spent most of yesterday together.

Simone had spent the day alone with only her thoughts for company.

They'd been decidedly dangerous thoughts.

Soon, Simone would call for coffee and then call to see if Gaby was awake and wanted her company, but for now she remained content to sit in her little guest-room courtyard, with the smell of night jasmine still lingering in the silvery dawn air.

She could do this.

No matter what Rafael's mood today, or her own mood for that matter, she would do this. For the brother she adored. For Gabrielle with whom she'd shared so many childhood dreams. For her own sake, because she would never forgive herself if she made a mess of the bridesmaid duties bestowed upon her.

She *could* control her longing for Rafael today. She just had to do something to take the edge off her need beforehand, that was all. Maybe she should have booked a dawn skydive or gone for a quick swim in shark-infested waters. Maybe she still could. How far away was the beach? She padded inside and looked at the tourist leaflet on the bench. The beach was hours away and there was no promise of sharks.

Fine, then, she would just have to think rural. Horses. A spirited stallion with a burning desire to remain un-broken. A wild, beautiful, big-hearted beast who refused every normal rule of engagement and all you had to do was forget the rein and earn his trust and trust him not to hurt you in return. That was if he ever let you get close enough to him to try. But if he did let you close…if he did let you ride…the experience stayed with you for ever and ruined you for all other horses.

'Bastard stallions,' she muttered. 'More trouble than they're worth.'

She could be good, this day. She could do her duty as Gabrielle's bridesmaid and her duty to the houses of Duvalier and Alexander both. One day. It wouldn't kill her to behave for one more day.

Then she would go to war.

'Your brother's been pacing my kitchen since 6:00 a.m.,' said Rafael, when Simone phoned the vineyard at Gabrielle's urging, ostensibly to get an update on Luc's frame of mind. 'I cooked half a pig, a leg of cow and a dozen eggs and he barely managed a slice of Vegemite on toast. That's gratitude for you.'

'Show him your winery,' said Simone.

'Done that.'

'I haven't seen you round these last couple of days,' she said next. Easy to be fearless from a distance. 'Inigo even asked if you were deliberately avoiding me—you know how people talk. He seemed to be under the impression that you might be afraid of me. Or something. And that would be a shame seeing as we're about to become one big happy family.'

Gabrielle snorted. Gabrielle grinned. Gabrielle silently shook her head.

'I'm not afraid of you, Simone,' Rafe said curtly. 'I'm not avoiding you. And I thought we had a truce for today.'

'Oh, we *do*,' she said earnestly. 'Has it started already?'

'It's today, isn't it?'

'Does that mean our truce finishes at midnight?'

Silence at that, followed by a curt one-word reply. 'No.'

'That's what I thought. Why don't we make this a twenty-four-hour truce starting from, say, now?'

'Fine.' If the phone could have bit her it would have.

'Perfect. So what are we going to do about my brother?'

'He's driving me almost as insane as you do.'

'Get him to help you make some wine,' she offered.

'I already have. Last night's vintage has been tried, tested, barrelled, and for evermore shall be known as Bride's Bane. It's quite a drop.'

'Luc better be sober, Rafael, or so help me you'll both pay.'

'Trust me, he's sober,' he said. 'But tell me this. What the hell am I supposed to do with him for another six hours?'

'You mean you don't have a plan?' Simone covered the phone with her hand and addressed Gabrielle in a loud whisper. 'Luc's fine. Completely relaxed. Not stressing at all.' She uncovered the handpiece and addressed the angelic man on the other end of the phone. 'Some best man you are.'

'I do have a plan,' he said. 'Bring the wedding forward five and a half hours and we'll meet you in the gazebo in twenty minutes. Luc likes it.'

'It'll never happen,' said Simone blithely. 'Take him to the barber's instead. The barber can give him a nice close shave.'

'No can do,' said Rafael. 'The days of the close shave are over. I'm the brother of the bride. This wedding's *on*. What say we meet you and Gabrielle for brunch? How's that for not avoiding you? You could come here. There's bacon.'

'No.'

'Lunch, then?'

'No.'

'I'll throw in some fried onions and BBQ sauce?'

'Feed that man fried onions today and I'll trim your grapevines to the ground and feed them to nameless ducks.'

'All right already,' he said with a long-suffering sigh. 'No need to labour the point. I'll name the ducks. Now where can we meet for lunch?'

'You are so sweet when you're desperate,' she said. She'd seen a golf course not far from the guest house. 'Take him for a game of golf.'

'Does he play golf?'

'He can learn.'

'Golf's a psychologically demanding game. I don't know that he should start learning it on his wedding day. It's unlikely to soothe him.'

'Then play poker. And put him on the phone.'

'Later.' Anyone would think Rafe actually wanted to talk to her. 'How's my sister this morning?'

'She's an oasis of radiance and calm.'

'Of course she is. Now try the truth.'

'Put it this way. Remind me to get married at dawn.'

'Are you sure you don't want to meet up for afternoon coffee at, say, three?'

'Your sister and I will be at the gazebo at six this evening. She'll be the one in the long white gown.' Simone rolled her eyes at Gabrielle who was laughing outright now. 'I'll be the one trailing behind her in the caramel-coloured sheath and, I promise you, we'll both be worth the wait.'

'I hate waiting,' he said.

Simone grinned. There was something about weddings and truces that appealed to the sadist in her. 'Don't we all.'

* * *

By five-thirty that afternoon, Gabrielle and Simone were gowned and groomed to radiant perfection, and Sarah had taken over fussing duty.

'Stop it,' said Sarah sternly as Simone bent to check the hem of Gabrielle's gown. 'It's my turn. From now on, you *both* get to stand there and look astonishingly beautiful and I get to do any last minute running around.'

The photographer arrived and started snapping. Harrison arrived and smiled shyly. Simone had met him earlier in the week—a big, spare-framed man with gentle strength, a rough-hewn face and eyes that were almost as blue as his son's. Rafe didn't resemble him much, apart from the colour of his eyes. Gabrielle's resemblance to Harrison was only slightly more pronounced. Both Rafe and Gaby were their mother's children when it came to startling good looks. But their hearts were true, and *that*, thought Simone, had more than a little to do with this man.

Harrison Alexander loved his children.

It was blindingly obvious from her conversations with Gabrielle that Harrison was their strongest supporter, and Simone wondered—not for the first time— what it was that had kept this man away from his children throughout their long and miserable childhood.

Josien hadn't allowed him access to them, obviously, but why?

Why hadn't he fought for them?

'Harrison!' Gabrielle didn't call him father, but the warmth of her smile and her outstretched hands proclaimed her love for this big, gentle man. 'You're looking very handsome.'

Harrison's bemused smile made it the truth. 'Trust me, I've got nothing on the best man and groom.'

'Except wisdom, experience, and charm,' murmured Simone. 'I bet you didn't spend the day trying to think of something to do to occupy your time until the wedding.'

'No, but I did remember a day like that, once,' confessed Harrison. 'I took pity on your brother and his groomsman and collected them up this morning. Every cow and calf I own has been herded from the far paddocks and into the cattle yards to the north. Tomorrow I'll shift them back.'

'You're a good man,' murmured Gabrielle, with a kiss for his weathered cheek.

'There was *some* method to my madness,' said Harrison. 'I'll probably drench them first.'

'Practical too,' said Simone admiringly. 'Those boys have *so* much to learn…' She fussed with a wisp of Gabrielle's hair, never mind Sarah's exasperated clucking. 'I do believe we're ready.'

'Daughter,' said Harrison gravely and extended his arm. 'If I may?'

'I love you,' said Gabrielle quietly. 'I'll always love you for what you've done for Rafael and for me. And yes, Father.' She placed her hand in the crook of his arm. 'You may.'

Simone's pleasure came in snatches after that. Gabrielle's laughter when she first spied the horse-drawn carriage and top-hatted coachman. Harrison handing them both up into the carriage before seating himself alongside the driver. The ripples of light reflected off the water of the tiny lake. The golden glow cast by the late afternoon sun. The day had held its promise and Simone would keep hers.

A truce.

'There he is,' said Gabrielle in a hushed voice.

'Yes.' There he was, standing right next to the groom. Simone allowed herself a moment's aching regret, just one, for what might have been, before putting that regret firmly behind her. 'There they are.'

'Courage, *mon amie*,' murmured Gabrielle.

'Today, I have plenty,' Simone assured her. 'Enough for you too if you need it.'

'I don't need it.'

'I know.' Simone smiled at the knowledge that Lucien's heart was for ever in safekeeping.

The photographer snapped more photos for the camera as they alighted from the carriage. Simone snapped more memories for her heart. The rich fragrance of autumn roses wafting up from the bridal bouquets. The glow of the old gold Duvalier pearls around Gabrielle's slender neck. Something borrowed, Simone had insisted. They'd belonged to Simone's mother, whose death had coloured both their lives. They were of Caverness and all that went with it, and they had endured, as the children of Caverness had endured.

Gabrielle wore them with love and with pride.

'You'll do,' whispered Simone as she inspected Gabrielle one last time before Harrison stepped into place to escort his daughter to the gazebo where Luc and Rafael waited. 'You'll do very nicely.'

Night and Day, the household staff used to call Luc and Rafael when they were children. So totally different, night to day, but each followed the other and always in perfect rhythm. Brothers of the heart and now brothers-in-law, and Simone was fiercely glad for Luc's sake that, through Gabrielle, Rafe would be drawn back into her brother's life.

Luc would be richer for it, and she…she would get by.

Simone barely heard the words of the ceremony. She knew they were beautiful. She knew them for truth. But she'd thrown her senses open, the better to catch the day and hold it close. Luc in his black tie regalia, so certain of his love for Gabrielle. Gabrielle incandescent with her love for him. And Rafael, who loved hard and never looked back, looked on in grave silence as he silently handed the safekeeping of his sister over to Luc.

An exchange of rings and then a kiss while Simone wrapped her calm around her like a shield and looked anywhere but at Rafael.

Congratulations and photos as the wedding party and guests made their way slowly through the gardens towards the restaurant. Simone held both bouquets now as the bride and groom greeted their guests. Many of Luc's friends and business associates had made the trip from Europe. Some hadn't had to travel quite so far. Simone kept a politician's eye open for future allies for the new Mrs Luc Duvalier. She kept a general's eye out for future enemies.

'What *are* you doing?' a deep and delicious voice murmured in her ear. 'Calculating the collective cost of every piece of jewellery in attendance?'

'Shh,' she said imperiously, resisting the urge to turn at once and look her fill. 'I'm counting.'

'Counting what?'

'Goodwill towards your sister.' She counted to five before turning to study Rafael, still only marginally prepared for the loss of breath that usually accompanied such a venture. 'For example—' yes…goodbye oxygen '—Melisandre Dubois does not have any. Such things are worth knowing.'

Rafe scanned the crowd. 'Point her out.'

'Black cocktail hat, strapless black bodice, long pink skirt.'

'Got her. Old flame of Luc's?'

'Please,' she said. 'Credit him with some intelligence. No, she's never been Luc's. She's a snob.'

Rafe's features hardened. 'Who else here is lacking in goodwill?' he said, and Simone told him. The children of Caverness guarded each other's backs. Some things never changed.

Inigo signalled discreetly from the restaurant entrance that it was time for the party to move inside. With a nod, Simone told Rafe and separately they worked the guests and made it happen.

Champagne flowed. Canapés were served on silver trays by circulating wait staff. Once the guests had settled and the champagne had begun to work its magic, Inigo announced the arrival of Mr and Mrs Luc Duvalier. They entered to generous applause and the strains of a lone violinist playing an unchained melody.

'I *love* what you've done with the roses,' Simone murmured to Inigo, who had moved to stand by the kitchen doors, the better to orchestrate seamless service.

'I *know*,' he said. 'Aren't they divine? But really, I only had to arrange them. Rafe was the one who scoured the state to find them.' Inigo eyed Rafael's fine form and offered up a theatrical sigh. 'It's such a waste.'

'Oh, I don't know,' said Simone as she caught Rafael's eye. Rafael knew they were studying him. He hadn't overheard them, but he was hazarding a pretty good guess as to the topic of their conversation and his eyes promised retribution of the dark and edgy kind. 'Not necessarily.'

Inigo smiled widely. 'Did you *see* that look he just

sent you? Call me a prophet but that's not a merciful look from a merciful man.'

'Mercy's not really one of his strengths,' said Simone and countered Rafael's displeasure with a smile of pure challenge. Common sense clearly wasn't one of hers.

'Ow!' said Inigo. 'Sweetheart, you really shouldn't poke at the man like that.'

'Have you ever met a man who can take you straight to hell and make you burn for more, Inigo?'

'No, but I'd like to. Send me a postcard. And don't be shy if there's anything I can do to help speed your impending trip into fiery oblivion. Cold water. Polar bears. Ice-train truck chains for restraining the vengeful angel over there, because seriously, my friend, he looks like he's planning on burning in hell right along with you.' Inigo shuddered theatrically. 'You just tell Uncle Inigo what you need.'

Rafael straightened his tie, gritted his teeth, and did his bit to make Luc and Gabrielle's guests feel welcome. It was an eclectic mix with figureheads of European winemaking dynasties mingling freely, and, to Rafael's eye, quite readily with their Australian counterparts. Luc had never met some of the wedding guests before. Gabrielle had never met most of them. It didn't seem to matter.

The reason it didn't seem to matter wore a muted coffee-coloured sheath, a smile that never dimmed, and wielded hostessing skills that commanded Rafe's respectful awe.

Poised and breathtakingly beautiful, and by dint of will and skill alone, Simone Duvalier merged the House of Duvalier and its associates with the House of Alexander.

Yes, it was true that Gabrielle and Rafael were the children of one of the most accomplished household estate managers in France, who up until recently had been in their employ.

Yes, indeed, Rafael had learned the art of making champagne from Simone's late father, but the red-grape blends had beguiled him in a different direction. Yes, it was champagne's loss—Simone's father had considered Rafael's champagne blends to be some of the finest the House of Duvalier had ever produced. In the last year of his life and as far as champagne was concerned, Phillipe had drunk *nothing* but the Caverness 1995 Special Reserve. It had been blended—under Phillipe's guidance—by Rafael when he was fifteen. Yes, indeed, collaboration might well take place again between Rafael and Luc.

But wait until you tasted Rafael's reds.

Gabrielle similarly, by way of Simone's expansion on Gabrielle's superior management and marketing skills, became a woman that Europe's winemaking elite could not readily or sensibly ignore. In between building the Alexander family name, Simone polished the House of Duvalier's reputation as a vibrant, progressive and wildly successful winemaking dynasty until it shone.

'She's a brilliant ambassador for them, isn't she?' murmured Gabrielle in one of the rare moments Rafe found himself alone with his sister.

'Where did she learn all this stuff?'

'Finishing school, on the job and at her father's side. Luc says that when you left she turned to her work. She'd sacrificed the man she loved for her role in the family business. Damned if she was going to make a mess of her business obligations too. Sound familiar?'

Rafael took the hit in silence. Gabrielle's expression softened.

'She loved you, Rafael. With all that she was. But she's loyal to her family too, and you left her nowhere to go. No workable solution whereby she could be with you and fulfil her family obligations as well. She couldn't leave, you couldn't stay. You can *see* how crucial she is to the running of the Duvalier winemaking empire.'

'I see it,' he said gruffly.

'I want to thank you. For showing Simone around the vineyard. For supporting her in her role as bridesmaid today. I knew you could do it.'

'Save it, angel,' he muttered. 'The night's still young.'

'I trust you,' she said and pressed a kiss to his cheek. 'Get to know her again, Rafe. For your own sake. She's a remarkable woman.'

That was what he was afraid of.

As far as Simone's extremely well-trained eye could see, everything was unfolding according to plan. The food was magnificent, they had ambrosia for wine, the setting was superb and the execution was flawless. Luc looked relaxed, Gabrielle divine, the guests appeared genuinely happy, and the formalities had been delivered in a mixture of languages and with a great deal of laid-back humour.

Harrison spoke fluent French, Dutch, German and passable Spanish and would prove a valuable addition to the future social events Simone had already started planning in her head.

Not your average Australian cattle farmer.

'Stop working,' said a dark, commanding voice as a tall glass of something that looked miraculously a lot like plain old iced water appeared in front of her. 'Relax for a moment. I'm getting exhausted just watching you. And here, take this. Inigo said to give it to you.'

Inigo was a fiend who'd clearly surrendered to the dark side.

But she took the glass from Rafe's outstretched hand and positioned him between her and the guests while she slaked her thirst for something without alcohol or bubbles in a most unladylike fashion.

She looked up on returning the glass to him to find that Rafe's vivid blue eyes had darkened and his body had grown still.

'I'm wondering which one's real,' he murmured. 'The wanton sensualist or the poised and confident hostess?'

'They both get a run every now and then,' she said. 'Which do you prefer?'

'Well, that would depend on where you were. And who you were with.'

'And were I alone with you in some dark secluded corner? Which would you choose then?'

'You *know* which one I'd choose, princess.'

'Actually, I don't.' She ignored the princess tag. For now. 'When I kissed you the other day you definitely didn't want wanton. You didn't want any part of it.'

He regarded her in brooding silence. 'I want to thank you for the build-up you gave the Alexander family tonight,' he said finally. 'I hardly recognised myself.'

Simone smiled. She'd embellished a little, but facts were facts. Rafael Alexander was a man to watch, both in business and for the sheer pleasure it afforded people to do so. 'It might take a while to secure Gabrielle's position as mistress of Caverness, but she's made a good start and you and Harrison have helped in no small measure by being charming, successful and socially adept. Of course, it doesn't hurt that you look like a fallen angel either.'

He smiled crookedly. 'Fallen?'

'Definitely. You don't have good boy written all over you, Rafael, and you know it.'

'Actually, I have "never look back" written all over me,' he murmured.

'Trust me,' she said. 'I hadn't forgotten.'

'Dance with me,' he said.

'That would require touching. And you know that's not a good idea.'

'Do it anyway,' he murmured. 'I can be good.'

She did it anyway, and settled tentatively into his arms. Her body thought it belonged there, but Simone begged to differ. They had an audience she'd been working all night and it wouldn't do to ruin all her good work now. So they danced the way friendly acquaintances danced, and she avoided Rafe's gaze and stamped down hard on her desire for more.

Gabrielle beamed at them. Luc shot Simone a warning glance. Careful, that glance said. Remember what became of this before.

She hadn't forgotten. Not the pleasure or the pain.

For now she concentrated on the little things. The feel of her hand resting lightly in Rafael's, his hand warm and slightly callused to the touch. His other hand at her back, assured, and taking no liberties. They had an audience to play and his sister's position in society to secure. Rafael knew this as well as she did and the truce held. Only as the dance ended did Rafe reveal the tiniest hint of battle readiness. His fingers brushed the inside of her wrist as he released her. One tiny discreet caress and her senses flamed to life.

Damn he was good when he was being bad.

The bride and groom left at midnight and Rafe—along with everybody else—saw them to the door and into the car Harrison had arranged for them. Harrison would take them to Angels Landing and then he would head on to his own home. Rafe had taken a room at the guest house for the night in order to give the newlyweds their privacy. All that was left for him to do now was bid farewell to the rest of the guests as they departed and then he too could leave, secure in the knowledge of a wedding relatively well handled.

He stayed by the door, seeing people out. Simone did the same, her graceful, charming presence a direct threat to his sanity and his strength of will. Finally, there was no one else left to say goodnight to apart from a handful of guests who'd moved to the bar and were keeping Inigo busy. Rafael figured them for gone, one way or another.

Which left him and Simone. She stood on the step, with darkness at her back and soft yellow light from the restaurant illuminating her exquisite face and turning her gown into a glowing, golden sheath.

'It's not over, you know,' she said quietly, and whether she spoke of the reception, their relationship or the truce he'd agreed to was anyone's guess, but she was right on all counts.

'I know,' he said gruffly. Would she resist if he reached for her and drew her into the shadow of the night? Would she offer him her mouth? He tried to block the memory of that mouth and the things it could do. Such a clever, busy mouth.

Simone's gaze turned dark and knowing and he knew before she spoke that she was about to acknowledge the beast that hungered inside him and invite it out to play, and she shouldn't. She really shouldn't.

'You should go back inside,' he murmured.

'You mean before I do something stupid?'

'Yes.'

She moved towards him swiftly, right up until the part where she set her lips to his and nipped at his lower lip with her teeth. That bit happened excruciatingly slowly.

It took a second, or maybe a minute, before he could trust himself to breathe. He could feel his control slipping, slipping through his fingers, and the harder he tried to hold onto it, the faster it disappeared.

'Go. *Now.*' His words cut at her and drove her to step away from him, as they were meant to.

'I won't offer again,' she said in the language of their youth.

A single snarling thought reared up from the dark places inside him, but he kept it to himself as she turned away and headed back inside.

She wouldn't need to.

Simone farewelled the guests at the bar, collected her evening bag, and, with the last remnants of her poise, made her way to the kitchen to thank the chef and the wait staff for their services. She had every intention of slipping out the kitchen's back door alone after that, but the chef had other ideas, stolidly insisting that a pair of his waiters walk her across the garden to her guest room.

'My room is two hundred metres away,' she protested laughingly. 'I'm hardly going to get lost.'

'It's dark,' said the gallant chef. 'You need an escort and if not my waiters then one of them can go and find Rafael. He can walk you across.'

'Have you and Inigo been plotting?' she said suspiciously.

'Inigo doesn't *plot*,' said the chef, with a jowly grin. 'He orchestrates. And here he is now, with your escort in tow. Never misses a beat.'

'Inigo says I should walk you across to your room,' said Rafael when he reached her.

'It's very dark,' said Inigo.

'And very late,' added the chef. 'You never know what you might find in the garden at this time of night. Territorial wombats…'

'Ten-foot wallabies,' said Inigo.

'Spider webs!' said the chef as if this would clinch the deal. 'We couldn't possibly send you on your way to the guest house alone.'

'Inconceivable,' said Inigo. 'Don't you *read* Agatha Christie? Fortunately, Rafael was just leaving. And might I just add, doesn't he look *divine* this evening?'

Rafael winced. Simone couldn't help the smile that crossed her lips or the encouragement of Inigo that sprang from them. 'Yes, indeed. Very handsome.'

'The breadth of shoulder,' said Inigo, warming to his subject. 'That face!'

'Any time you're ready,' murmured Rafael.

'Wait!' said Inigo, scanning the chef's collection of kitchen-shelf dessert liqueurs and reaching for the Frangelico. He handed it to Rafael. 'Nightcap.'

'Nice touch,' said the chef. 'Although I'd have given him the Cognac.'

'There's the nicest secluded garden nook, about halfway to the house,' said Inigo. 'Perfect for—'

'*Move,*' said Rafael and Simone hastily complied and headed for the door.

A chorus of farewells followed their departure, the kitchen door closed behind them, and night air wrapped around them, cool and dewy after the warmth of the day.

'You don't have to—'

'Stop,' he said sharply. 'I don't want to hear it.'

Simone stopped. Searched for conversation that would assure him that she'd not embarrass him with yet another unwanted advance. 'Have you been in contact with Etienne de Morsay again?'

'Yes. I put him off. Gabrielle was adamant about not wanting him to come here.'

'Really? Did she say why?'

'No.' Rafael ran an impatient hand through his hair. 'Not exactly. Nothing that made sense, at any rate. I'm meeting him in Sydney tomorrow. Hopefully, I'll get some answers then.'

Simone chewed thoughtfully on her lower lip. 'Did you ask Luc about him?'

'No.'

'You should have.'

'He was a little preoccupied, Simone.'

'Though he still had time to make wine, eat a manly breakfast and muster cattle before heading out to get married.'

'Exactly.'

Simone hitched up her gown a fraction to keep it off the grass. Bridesmaid gowns weren't really designed for grass.

'Princess,' he murmured.

'Practical,' she corrected smoothly.

'It suits you,' he said reluctantly. 'The gown. The colour. Whatever you've done with your hair.'

'Was that a *compliment*?'

'Yes.' Rafael glared at her.

Simone glared back. 'Thank you.'

This time, he looked away. 'I never really realised before tonight, exactly how much I asked you to give up for me,' he said after they'd walked in silence for a while.

'You mean my position in European society?' Simone judged the risks involved with continuing with this line of conversation. The risk of further quarrelling was high. The chance of her and Rafael resolving their issues was low. She went ahead and plunged into the heart of things anyway. 'I'd have given it up in a heartbeat for you, Rafael. But I had my father and Luc to consider as well, and in the end I couldn't abandon them. They needed me.'

'More than I needed you?'

She'd wanted this, Simone reminded herself grimly. This clearing of the air, never mind that the mirror he held up to her actions revealed her in an ugly light.

'You needed to escape the chains that bound you to Caverness. You burned to make your own way in life, and you have. What had I to offer you, Rafael? Tell me that? An unbreakable link to a place you never wanted to return to and not one single skill that would come in useful outside of the niche that had been created for me.'

'You underestimate yourself.'

'Maybe I did. And maybe I realise that now. But I was eighteen, Rafael, and I was scared. You were my heart. Caverness was my home. And my duty lay with the House of Duvalier. I could not have all three. Right or wrong, I chose to stay. You chose to leave.'

'I *had* to leave,' he said curtly.

'I know that,' she said. 'Josien... I know how she treated you... I knew you only stayed as long as you did in order to protect Gabrielle from her rages. I always knew you'd leave. I've never blamed you for that.'

'I blamed you,' he said. 'Hell, I blamed you for everything. It got me through the early days of being alone.'

'Happy to help,' she said faintly.

His lips twisted. 'I don't know where I'm going with this, Simone. I don't know what I want from you. Anger. Absolution. Affection. I've got *no* idea.'

That made two of them. 'You know what I thought when Gabrielle told me the wedding would be held in Australia and that you were to be Luc's best man?' she said tentatively. 'I thought that finally, *finally*, I might be able to make my apologies and move on. I wanted to let go of the thought of you.' They'd reached her tiny courtyard. 'I wanted to stop measuring every man I met against you.'

'And have you?' he asked quietly as he leaned against the wall, nightcap in one hand and watchfulness in his eyes.

'Well, I certainly have a new measure of man in place.' Unfortunately, it was still firmly based on him. 'Whether it serves me any better than the old one remains to be seen.' Simone fished the key to the sliding door from her evening bag and went about unlocking it and sliding the door wide open. Surrendering her shoes at the door, Simone slipped inside, not daring to turn and see if Rafael had followed her.

She switched on the dining-room lamp, belatedly remembering that she'd left the room in a shambles and that the dining table had been awash with morsels of food meant to tempt Gabrielle into eating something before the ceremony. It wasn't awash with food any more. Someone, probably the magnificent Sarah, had whisked it all away and tidied up in the process. 'How do you think Sarah, Inigo, and the chef would feel about relocating to France?' she asked, only half in jest.

'I think Deidre who owns the guest house would shoot you.' Rafael had ventured inside after all. Heaven help them both.

'Just checking.' Simone's mouth suddenly felt very dry as Rafael set the Frangelico down on the counter and headed for the refrigerator. He found the jug of water and poured some into a tall glass. He poured one for her too. It sat there on the counter, untouched, a decision she did not want to make for fear that she would get it wrong. Princess or wanton? She could be either, and sometimes both, but Rafael did not want the wanton. No. For all his mockery, it was the princess he responded to. The princess who'd earned his compliments, and so it was that the princess stood before him now, trying desperately to appear composed and in control of her wayward emotions.

'Are you heading off in the morning?' he said.

'Yes. Yes, to Sydney for a day before I fly out.' She hadn't wanted to linger. Not with Gabrielle and Luc gone and this so very clearly Rafael's territory.

'Whereabouts in Sydney?'

'The Four Seasons.'

He nodded. 'Will you be able to find it okay?'

'The car has GPS.'

He nodded again. Conversation stalled. It was time to let go. Time to start dreaming of a life without an angel in it, avenging or otherwise.

Simone stepped woodenly towards him and held out

her hand. She would weep once he'd gone but right now she gave him what he wanted and played the princess as she said goodbye. 'Good luck with Etienne tomorrow.'

He looked at her and something flickered behind his eyes. He ignored her hand. Put the tips of his fingers to her cheek and kissed her softly on the lips. 'That's for the princess who helped make my sister's wedding day a memorable one.'

Her lips clung; she couldn't help it. He meant too much to her, this man, and always had.

Rafael's gaze sought hers, searing and tormented as his hand slid around to the back of her neck and he tilted her head, his lips hovering millimetres above her own. 'Damn you,' he whispered raggedly. 'Damn you to hell, because this is for me.'

And then his lips crushed down on hers as he unleashed his passion and his fury, all of it, all at once, and dragged her with him to a place where a dark and sensual madness ruled them both.

He wanted her wanton and naked before him. He wanted to possess her until she convulsed around him and screamed out his name. Heaven help him, he wanted to break her, and remake her, and scar her soul the way she'd scarred his. 'Say you want what only I can give you,' he murmured as he backed her against the counter and his lips found hers again and then her cheek, and then the vulnerable spot behind her ear. '*Say* it.'

'I do want it,' she whispered, her hands inside his jacket, her fingers seeking the buttons on his vest, and then the shirt, and then her hands slid to his chest as she dragged her lips across his throat. 'All of it.' His jacket fell to the floor. He found the zipper of her dress and slid it south. Flesh, warm and fragrant. Softness and curves and a taste he'd never forgotten. Urgency, and madness as he finally got her naked and lifted her in his arms the better to take what he wanted and he wanted it all.

Flesh cleaved to flesh and lips upon lips as she gave and he took without care for the price.

A bed and some sheets and Simone in his arms, crying out his name as he buried himself deep inside her, one hand on the curve of her behind as he positioned her exactly where he wanted her and, with his heart pounding and his soul fighting to be free of its cage, began to move.

'Slower,' she whispered as her body responded instantly, hot and slick and tightening as she spoke. 'It's been too long for me. Rafael, please. You have to slow down or I won't last a minute.'

He didn't want her to. He wasn't asking her to. 'Say my name.' He wanted her screaming, he wanted it now, and, calling on the ruthlessness that always lingered just below the surface, he sought her centre with his thumb and stroked. '*Say* it.'

She cried out as she came for him, a ragged word escaping her lips, a broken word, both curse and plea. She clawed at him to join her and he did, tumbling down after her, over her, as he gave himself up to unbearable pleasure and to hell with the pain that would come of it.

Simone surfaced hard from the depths of pleasure, gasping as tiny aftershocks rocked her body. Pleasure flowed, desire consumed, and Rafael's touch gentled as he rolled to one side, still cradling her tightly in his arms.

He gave her no words, there were no words for this.

But touch, he gave her that, and the thundering of his heart beneath her cheek, he gave her that too.

'Are you protected?' he said gruffly.

'From pregnancy? Yes.' From losing her heart to this man all over again? She feared not. Simone eased up onto one elbow the better to study him. Rafe's eyes glittered in the dim light, so boldly blue and almost sated. His lips curved as she slid over him and settled on top of him more fully, her hands either side of his head as her hair fell across one shoulder to curtain them both. 'I want to spend the night with you,' she said as her lips brushed his jawline.

'Yes.'

'The whole night.'

'Yes.' He drew her down for another kiss. *Not* sated, that kiss told her. Not nearly.

Good.

She let his possession of her mouth inflame her. She let the feel of his body beneath hers consume her. The hard and rippling planes of his chest. She wanted to go slow this time, to record and to remember, and, wordlessly, he made the world turn slow as he rebuilt the flames of desire caress by deliberately slow caress.

Only when she was on the brink of ecstasy did he enter her and with unerring certainty drive her once more towards oblivion; that place where the world fell away and there was only one anchor and his name was Rafael.

Rafael dozed in the aftermath of Simone's lovemaking. He wanted to remain awake the better to remember every moment, but with his body urging him towards sleep and with Simone already embracing it, he knew he'd soon surrender to the pull of night. Rafe knew how to live in the moment. He knew how to seize it.

Keeping it was the hard part.

One hand above his head and his other around the only

woman he'd ever loved with all that he was. The only woman he'd ever exposed his scarred but steadfast soul to.

It hadn't been enough.

His love for her. His dreams of a future together if only she would believe in him, and *be* with him. His confidence in her love for him.

It hadn't been enough.

Simone had stayed on at Caverness, Rafael had stormed away in anger and in grief, and, *God*, it hurt to look back. *Don't* look back. Don't ever look back.

He closed his eyes and willed sleep to come.

There was nothing there he wanted to see.

CHAPTER FIVE

MORNING came too soon for Simone.

'No,' she murmured when Rafael shifted restlessly beside her. A half-asleep protest as she opened her eyes and realised the advent of the day. She closed her eyes tightly and rolled onto her stomach as she reached for the pillow to fill the space Rafael had just vacated. 'No.'

'Shower,' he said huskily. 'Care to join me?'

'No.' And then with one eye cautiously open... 'Maybe.'

His smile was lazy. His eyes were bold. 'Suit yourself.'

He left and closed the bathroom door behind him. The shower came on. The sheets came off. Simone had never been one to linger in bed when a challenge had been issued. She recalled with a tiny smile the firm hardness of every bit of Rafael's lean and luscious body.

Challenge had most certainly been issued.

She almost chickened out as she stood on one side of the glass shower door with Rafael and a cascade of steaming water on the other. And then the door slid open and a hand reached for her and dragged her inside and that was the end of that.

'You're very decisive,' she murmured. 'It's irritatingly appealing.'

He smiled a devil's smile as he pinned her against the cubicle wall. 'I know. Come with me today. To Sydney. I'll get someone else to drive your hire car back.'

She wanted to. Badly. But caution had arrived with the day. Bedding Rafael had solved none of the issues hovering between them. Okay, maybe it had solved one, but the rest remained in place.

'The meeting with Etienne won't take long,' he said next. 'You could come along, and then afterwards I'll show you Sydney.'

She slid from his grasp, stalling for time, as she stood beneath the spray. 'Will you show me where you got your tattoo?'

His eyes grew shadowed. 'No.'

'Turn around,' she ordered next, and pushed and prodded until she had Rafael where she wanted him, with his head flung back and his arms raised, hands resting on the tiles as water ran in rivulets down his back, over the words and the picture she'd striven so hard to forget.

'I hate you for this,' she murmured, tracing the darkened words that flowed across his back with the tips of her fingers, before finally pressing her mouth to the ink that graced his shoulder blade. 'I love you for it too.'

Pleasure and pain. More pleasure than pain as he turned and thrust his hand into her hair and kissed her hard. They wouldn't make it out of the shower before he took her again, she knew that much already.

She wouldn't make it through the day without sacrificing her heart. She knew that too.

'Show me your Sydney, then,' she murmured as the last of her resistance to this man was crushed beneath the feel of his hands on her. 'I'll give you this day.'

* * *

They made it to Sydney with half an hour to spare before Rafael's meeting with Etienne. By the time they'd parked the car underground and Rafael had caught her and kissed her as she got out of the car, and they'd made it to the lifts and into the foyer of the hotel, and found the washrooms and freshened their appearances, they only had five minutes to spare.

Being five minutes early to a meeting with a reigning monarch who wanted to offer you a plum commission wasn't such a bad thing, she assured Rafael laughingly, before asking him yet again if he thought she would be in the way.

'I've never met the man before, Simone. He's known you since childhood. You won't be in the way.'

Etienne had chosen to meet Rafael for lunch in the restaurant attached to the hotel. He stood as they approached him. A big, spare-framed man, immaculately attired in a dark suit and shirt. A man with a handsome face and a brilliant blue gaze that fixed on Rafael and never wavered.

Simone stopped abruptly, sucker punched into immobility.

Comprehension dawned.

Etienne's knowledge of Rafael's achievements. Gabrielle's insistence that Etienne stay away. Not from the vineyard, but from *Rafael*. 'Oh, no.' She shook her head. 'No.'

Rafael had stopped too, his eyes on her, puzzled and questioning. 'Simone? What is it?'

'Rafe—'

'What is it? What's wrong?'

'I don't...I can't...' She shook her head, trying to clear it. 'Maybe you shouldn't...'

'Shouldn't what?' His words echoed her unspoken ones.

'Let's just forget this meeting and go,' she implored him.

'Go where?'

'Anywhere!' Anywhere but towards Etienne de Morsay, who was currently heading towards them. 'Rafael, *please*. I'm…I'm feeling unwell. Please, let's just go.'

Rafe slid his hand beneath her elbow and frowned. 'How unwell?'

The lies were making her sick to her stomach. Her distress must have shown on her face.

'Okay,' he said hurriedly. 'A room. We'll get you a room where you can lie down. Let me make our apologies to de Morsay.'

'No!'

'No to *what*?'

Simone was fast making a spectacle of herself. Rafael looked to be fast losing patience. Etienne was fast approaching. Maturity fled as she reverted to childhood and tugged urgently on Rafael's arm. 'Run,' she said pleadingly. 'Rafael, *run*.'

And then Etienne was holding out his hand and Rafael was taking it, shaking it, as blue eyes met blue and Simone watched in white-knuckled silence. And then Rafael was making their apologies and saying that she was unwell and two sets of concerned blue eyes were upon her and Simone looked from one to the other and prayed to the gods that this was all just a dream and knew that it was not.

'Here,' said Rafael gently and herded her towards a chair. 'Sit for a little, while I see to a room.'

Rafael *run*, her mind screamed at him. 'Yes,' she said

threadily, and then in a stronger voice as her mind began to function. 'Yes, but I already have a room booked somewhere.' She fumbled in her handbag for the details. 'I just need to get there.' She just needed to get Rafael there. Anywhere but here.

'I have a suite here,' Etienne was saying. 'It's closer. Please, it's at your disposal.'

'You're very…' She would choke on the word *kind* if she uttered it. Where had this man been during Rafael's childhood? Where the *hell* had he been when Josien was whipping the light out of her son in punishment for imaginary wrongs? 'I can't…'

'A glass of water, then,' said Etienne and almost as soon as he said the words one was being pressed into her hand. She grasped it and drank deeply. Rafael's eyes warmed and his lips tilted upwards. 'Hoyden,' he murmured as he brushed her temple with his lips. 'Feeling a little better?'

She set the glass down on the table. 'Yes.' No. But she would recover and shield Rafael as best she could from this man. She had to.

She turned to the reigning king of Maracey. 'My apologies, Your Highness. And my belated greetings.'

Etienne waved her apology away with a flick of his hand and offered up a charming smile and she winced inside because she knew that smile, she knew it well, and had never once made the connection. Until now.

'You used to call me Etienne, young Simone,' he said. 'Would that you do so again.'

'Thank you, Your Highness.' But she would rot in hell before she would claim any kind of friendship with this man. She stood on wobbly legs.

'My suite, I think,' said Etienne.

'No,' she said. 'The dizziness has passed. I'm okay.'

'Are you sure?' Rafael was in front of her now, blocking out Etienne's image. Remaking it.

'Oh, Rafael.' Her heart wept for the lies that surrounded him. How long had Gabrielle known? Did Luc know? Harrison *had* to know. Didn't he?

'We won't stay long,' he murmured. 'Sit for a few minutes and make sure you're really feeling okay, and then we'll go.'

Simone summoned a smile and called on years of social conditioning to get her through these next few minutes. 'Of course.'

Etienne saw them seated at his table, calling immediately for more water, and some fruits and an array of food to nibble on. 'To lift your energy levels,' he said. 'My late wife often took dizzy spells early in her pregnancies. Food always helped.'

'I'm not pregnant,' said Simone, glancing at Rafe from between her lashes to see how he had reacted to Etienne's statement. 'And your wife. Mariette. I was sorry to hear that she'd passed away. She was a remarkable woman.'

'Yes, she was. Alas, she never carried a child to term. It was not to be,' said Etienne.

'A pity.' Simone lifted her chin and stared at the monarch. She thought she knew where Etienne was heading with this conversation. Why he was being so frank about his so-called 'childless' state. But he would have to go through her to get there. 'Rafael mentioned that you're looking to restore a vineyard,' she said smoothly.

'Yes, I am.'

'A passing interest, is it?'

'A long-awaited project,' Etienne countered politely. 'It's been on my mind for years.'

'A pity you never managed to *get* to it years ago,' she said sweetly. 'Sometimes it's just too late.'

'Time will tell.' Etienne turned to Rafael. 'Of course, I don't expect anyone to take on such a project, sight unseen. I'm hoping to persuade you to come and view the vineyard for yourself.'

'And what of Rafael's own vineyard commitments?' snapped Simone. 'Do you expect him just to drop them, so as to accommodate your every whim?'

'Simone,' murmured Rafael, shooting her a sharp glance, accompanied by the slight shake of his head.

'You have many champions, *señor*,' murmured Etienne.

'So it seems.' Not that Rafael had the foggiest notion as to *why* Simone had seen fit to leap to his defence. He didn't need it. He could see no reason for her antagonism towards her father's old friend. 'But Simone is correct in that regard. Any project I undertook for you would have to fit in around my own schedule.'

The look Simone sent de Morsay was darkly triumphant and in no way friendly. Etienne swallowed it down whole, with a rueful smile. First Gabrielle, and now Simone. What was it about Etienne de Morsay that upset them so? Rafael had seen Simone's formidable social skills in play at the wedding. She wasn't using them now.

'Rafael, I'd like to leave,' she said. 'Now.'

'In a minute.' Rafael turned to Etienne. 'I have no reputation as a winemaker within your part of the world. Frankly, I'm still building a reputation in *my* part of the world. I'm curious about how you came to hear of me.'

'I've always known about you, Rafael.'

'No,' said Simone, white-faced as she pushed to her feet and confronted Etienne. 'You can't *do* this.'

'Needs must,' said Etienne quietly, rising from his chair and executing a slight bow. Anyone looking on would have thought it nothing more than a courtly gesture. Rafael didn't know what to think, but he stood as well.

'Whose needs?' Had Simone been a cat she would have spat at him. 'Yours?'

'The monarchy demands it.'

'I care *nothing* for your monarchy.'

'So I see. Some days I don't care much for it either.' The older man's shoulders sagged and he seemed to age at least ten years. He turned towards Rafael, every weary movement a silent apology. 'I had hoped to do this differently,' he murmured. 'But every other avenue was closed to me. I want you to know that.'

'Speak your piece,' said Rafael. He had a bad feeling about this. Simone's open hostility. Gabrielle's alarm when he'd mentioned Etienne de Morsay. De Morsay's vivid blue eyes drilling holes in Rafael. There was something familiar about him. Something Rafael struggled to place.

He watched in silence as the older man drew himself upright. Finally, he spoke.

'My name is Etienne de Morsay. Husband to Mariette Sulemon of the Ardennes—lately deceased. Son of Francisco de Morsay—also deceased. Grandson of Pieter. Great grandson of Alain. I am reigning monarch of the territory of Maracey, bordered by Spain, and you, Rafael Francisco Pieter Alexander, are my son.'

Rafael stared at him. Hard. Those eyes. That big, sparse frame. Heaven help him, that face. He saw an echo of that face, that frame, and those eyes every morning when he looked in the mirror. He shook his head. No.

'Yes,' said Etienne.

'No. Harrison Alexander is my father.'

'No,' said Etienne gently.

Rafael took the blow in silence. Such a deep and destructive blow. Did Harrison know? Did Gabrielle? The knife inside him tightened. Gabrielle had known. And Simone...Simone had known too. Anger took hold, brutal and burning as he turned towards her and saw knowledge in her eyes. 'You knew.' His voice shook. His pain roared. 'You *knew.*'

'No.' She looked to be on the verge of tears. He was so *sick* of women and their tears and their duplicity.

'You knew. That's why my company suddenly became acceptable after all these years of silence. *That's* why you deigned to spend time in my bed. You thought I was a goddamn prince!'

'*No!* Rafael, I swear—'

'You wanted to leave,' he said harshly. 'So leave.'

Simone stared at him, dark stricken eyes in an unnaturally pale face as she reached out a hand towards him. 'That's not how it was.'

'Don't,' he said sharply. If she touched him, he would break. 'Don't *touch* me. Just go.'

'You're a fool, Rafael Alexander Pieter whoever the hell you are,' she said raggedly as she dropped her hand and reached for her handbag instead. She drew herself up with a glittering gaze that accompanied both him and de Morsay. 'Both of you, fools.'

He watched her stalk away, beautiful in her anger, the emptiness left by her departure fuelling his.

'You shouldn't have done that,' said the man beside him.

'Who the hell asked you?' Anger found a new target, the right target, this time. 'Who are you to tell me what

I should do?' Anger ruled him. Despair rode him. 'Let me tell you something, you right royal bastard. You're no father of mine. I don't care what you can prove by blood. I don't know you. I don't care about you. And I have no intention of *ever* being your son.'

Simone's luggage was gone from the car by the time the valet brought it around to the front of the hotel. She'd collected it not ten minutes ago, the hotel employee told Rafe. She'd had the doorman call for a taxi. She had seemed to be in something of a hurry. The young valet eyed Rafael anxiously, as if sensing something of the roiling emotions beneath the contained façade.

The young valet paled and his Adam's apple bobbed as he swallowed hard and asked Rafe if he'd done the right thing.

'That's fine. No problem,' muttered Rafael before retrieving the keys and heading for his car. He knew the name of the hotel Simone was booked into. He knew what time her flight would leave the following day. He could have found her. Talked to her. Gone to her.

He didn't.

For all that Simone had known—or guessed—Etienne's connection to him, she wasn't guilty of the subterfuge that had created this mess. Josien was. Josien, who'd hated him every day of her miserable life and he finally knew why. Bastard son of a prince who'd abandoned her.

Bastard boy with his father's eyes and his father's colouring and God knew what else he'd inherited from the man. Arrogance and ambition that Josien had done her utmost to beat out of him. His burning need for independence. His fierce and cold intelligence. Had all that come from Etienne de Morsay too?

Who knew?

Josien would know, but Josien was dead to him. More so now than ever.

Gabrielle had known. Somehow, Gabrielle had known, and hadn't seen fit to tell him. The pain of that betrayal cut deep.

And then there was Simone... Rafael closed his eyes to block out the image of Simone's first frantic attempts to prevent his meeting with de Morsay. Those final whispered words before the older man had walked up to them. Run, she'd whispered, and catapulted him straight back to their childhood. *Rafael, run.*

Simone *hadn't* known of his true relationship with Etienne de Morsay beforehand. Oh, she'd guessed soon enough. The minute she'd seen them together in the same room her formidable brain had probably started connecting the dots. But she hadn't put it together before then.

De Morsay was right. When it came to Simone's part in all of this, he'd been a fool.

He almost turned the car around then. He almost went back for her, such was his need to talk with her and take comfort from her and try and make all the jagged shards of his life fit together the way he wanted them to fit.

He didn't.

Maybe if he'd been a little more trusting he might have turned back.

He didn't.

Harrison stood waiting for him on the verandah of Rafael's house when Rafael finally pulled the car up beside it, several hours later. One look at the older man's worn face and weary eyes and the heart Rafael had been holding together with a piece of string finally shattered.

He left the car and headed for the door, ignoring Harrison at first as he attempted instead to push the house key into its lock. It wouldn't go in. His hand shook too much and it wouldn't go in.

'You knew.' He still couldn't look at the older man. He looked at his hands instead and fisted them tight. 'You knew I wasn't yours.'

'Yes, I knew.' Harrison's voice came low and strained. 'You were born seven months after my wedding day, Rafael. A perfectly healthy, full-term baby boy. I didn't know who had sired you, but I did know that you couldn't have been mine. I didn't care.'

'How could you not *care*?'

'You were an innocent child, Rafael. What would you have had me do? Turn you away?'

'I wasn't yours.'

'And I loved you anyway, and always, as if you were mine. A heart can do that, you know. Love beyond measure something that doesn't belong to you.'

Rafael's throat closed up tight.

'When Josien left and took you and Gabrielle with her, she broke my heart,' said Harrison in that quiet melodic way of his that Rafael had always loved. 'When she refused to allow me access to you on the grounds that I wasn't your father, she broke it twice over.'

'Gabrielle…' Rafael finally found his voice and pushed it past the constriction in his throat. 'Is Gabrielle…?'

'Gabrielle's mine,' said Harrison. 'But to fight for her I would have had to abandon you, separate your sister from you, and I couldn't do it.'

Rafael put his cheek to the smooth, worn weatherboard and closed his burning eyes.

'The day you turned up on my doorstep was one of

the happiest days of my life,' said Harrison quietly. 'The day Gabrielle arrived was the other.'

Rafael put his hands to the wall, his eyes still tightly closed. He wanted the boards to be cold to the touch. Why weren't they cold? Grown men did not sink to the floor and weep.

'Two hours ago I got a phone call from a man who claimed to be your father, and a king, and heaven knows what else. I don't know what caused him to walk away from Josien and from you all those years ago, but I do know that where you were concerned it was his loss. And my gain.'

Harrison moved closer. A large, warm hand came to rest tentatively on Rafael's shoulder.

'This man, this king, he wishes to meet with you again. He argued strongly for my support in the matter. He spoke of matters of state, and inheritance and regret. I told him I would speak with my son and that we would get back to him with an answer.'

'I don't know what to do,' whispered Rafael. A cry from the heart while his soul silently wept.

'That makes two of us,' said Harrison. 'But know this, Rafael. No matter what revelations lie ahead, I will think of you as mine and I will always stand by you. Always.'

They stood like that for a very long time before Rafael finally gathered the courage to speak of other things that had happened during the day.

'I hurt a woman today, Papa. I hurt a woman whose only crime was to care for me and to try and protect me.'

Harrison took the keys from him. Harrison opened the door to the house. 'Well…hell, son.' Harrison's words came delivered with a thread of dusty humour, drier than drought. 'No one ever said loving you was easy.'

CHAPTER SIX

HAVING Gabrielle and Luc back from their honeymoon and staying at Caverness while they made plans to restore the nearby Hammerschmidt house and vineyard brought both pleasure and sorrow to Simone. The pleasure lay in enjoying their company and in watching the love that flowed between them. The sorrow came when Gabrielle would speak to her of Rafael and what was happening in his fast-changing world.

Rafael had gone to Maracey, Gabrielle had told her. Rafael and Harrison both, at Etienne de Morsay's invitation, although Harrison had since returned to Australia. How it had all come about, Gabrielle never said, but apparently Etienne was making no secret of the fact that Rafael was his son and that, henceforth, Rafael would be an integral part of Etienne's life.

How the world did turn.

Simone arrived early at the village café Gabrielle had chosen for their mid-morning distribution meeting, and quickly ordered mineral water and a slice of fresh-baked baguette, no butter, no accompaniments, just the bread. Gabrielle arrived moments later and added more bread and water to the order, along with a decaf skinny latte, no sugar and no cocoa on top.

'Seriously,' said Simone after the waiter had retreated with their order. 'Why have one?'

'Habit,' said Gabrielle with a grin. 'This pregnancy business is no fun at all when it comes to what you can and can't eat. No soft cheese, no wine, no coffee, minimal tea, easy on the chocolate. There's nothing left on my favourites list at all.'

'I hear spinach is good,' said Simone and chuckled when Gabrielle levelled her with a glance.

'I noticed you took no wine at dinner last night,' said Gabrielle, thumping her work folder on the table and making the cutlery jump.

'Headache,' said Simone briefly.

'Or the night before.'

'Two headaches,' said Simone. 'Two headaches and an unexpected yen for a teetotal life. Don't tell my distributors.'

'I hear you're handing over more of your distribution work to your second in command, not to mention the stuff you're handing on to me,' said Gabrielle next.

'If you didn't want the work you shouldn't have asked for it,' said Simone, grateful for the sunglasses that hid her eyes from Gaby's searching gaze.

'I want it,' said Gabrielle simply. 'What does intrigue me these days is that you don't. You spend every spare moment walking in your gardens or working in them. Luc's worried about you, Simone, and so am I. If having a pair of newlyweds around you at Caverness is a problem for you, I want you to *say* something.'

'It's not a problem.' Simone smiled and reached out her hand. Gabrielle covered it with hers instantly. 'I love having you at Caverness. And I love seeing you and Luc so happy.'

'Thank you,' said Gabrielle with a warm smile. 'Although it does leave me with this theory that I shared with Luc last night about the possible reason for your current life choices. He thought it a little far-fetched.' Gabrielle shook her head. 'Men.'

The food arrived. Two glasses of water, the joyless coffee, and two half slices of bare bread.

'I rest my case,' murmured Gabrielle. 'You've lost weight. You're not eating the things you usually enjoy…'

'I'm dieting,' murmured Simone.

'Well, you shouldn't be,' said Gabrielle bluntly. 'Not in your condition.'

Simone picked up her water and sipped.

Gabrielle sat back, clearly frustrated. 'You're going to make me ask who the father is, aren't you?'

'Not at all,' Simone murmured.

'So you'll tell me without prompting?'

'No.'

'I hate this,' said Gabrielle. 'I hate being right, and knowing I'm right, and knowing you don't trust me enough to confide in me.'

'All right.' Simone took a deep breath and set her glass gently on the table. 'I'm pregnant.'

'Finally.' Gabrielle did not look smug. She looked concerned. 'Have you seen a doctor?'

'Yes.'

'And everything is okay?'

'Yes.'

'And how far along are you?'

'Ten weeks.'

Gabrielle sighed heavily. 'God, I hate being right.'

No more than Simone hated being proved reckless, and thoughtless and stupid. She'd thought her low-dose pills would protect her. They hadn't.

'You have to tell him,' said Gabrielle next.

'Tell who?'

'Don't give me that.' Gabrielle shot her an icy reprimand. 'My brother. Rafael. Used to give you head starts in running races and the occasional frog. CEO of Angels Landing Wines. Son of Josien. Son of Harrison. Son of Etienne. Heir to the throne of bloody Maracey. Oh, and father of your unborn child.'

'It's not Rafe's fault that he ended up son of Etienne and heir to Maracey,' Simone felt compelled to utter in his defence. 'That one came as a complete surprise.'

'And yet, strangely, I still want to strangle him,' said Gabrielle. 'Has he contacted you since the wedding?'

'No.' Simone looked away as her heart constricted. 'I don't expect him to. We shared one night, Gabrielle. It meant nothing to him.'

'Well, it produced something,' said Gabrielle curtly. 'You have to tell him.'

'Don't you think he's had enough responsibilities thrust upon him for the time being?'

'I don't care what responsibilities he's had thrust upon him,' snapped Gabrielle. '*This* responsibility is one he brought upon himself! For heaven's sake, Simone. Do you *want* this child to grow up without ever knowing its father? Do you *want* this baby's childhood to echo Rafael's?'

'I *love* this baby,' said Simone fiercely. 'And he will *never* have a childhood like Rafael's.'

Gabrielle slumped back into her seat, tears streaming from her eyes. 'Bloody hormones,' she said shakily, wiping them away.

'It's not the hormones.'

'You're right. It's my overprotective friend and my foolish brother who are making me weep.' Gabrielle picked up her coffee with both hands and sipped. 'Would you like my opinion? As your friend and as Rafael's sister?'

Simone nodded.

Gabrielle looked troubled. 'Okay, here it is. I appreciate that Rafael has a lot on his plate right now. I appreciate that *you* appreciate that, but there's no way around this, Simone, and it's not going to get any easier. You have to tell him.'

'I will.' Simone's hand shook as she reached for her bread. 'Soon.' As soon as she'd gathered the courage for it. 'But not just yet.'

Etienne's vineyard estate was a forbidding stone fortress, built in the Spanish style. Older than Caverness, it cut across the hillside and stood sentry over the valley below. Rafael hadn't wanted to feel comfortable here. He hadn't wanted the beauty of the land and the stark splendour of the fortress to get to him, but the undeniable fact was that it had.

He liked this place.

Etienne had wanted him to stay at the palace in the capital, but Rafael had resisted taking up residence there. The vineyard Etienne was paying him to oversee the restoration of was here. He didn't need to stay at the palace. He didn't want to stay there.

The papers had been full of pictures of him and Etienne from the moment he'd set foot in Maracey. The resemblance had been unmistakable. A simple palace announcement had taken care of the rest.

Maracey, please meet Rafael Alexander de Morsay, son of Etienne.

The press had gone wild.

Sinner or saint. It depended which paper you read.

Apparently, he had the face for either and the background for both.

Rafael smiled grimly. He'd been here for a month and he'd thrown himself into the work of restoring Etienne's vines. Occasionally, Etienne would request the pleasure of his company at a state dinner or function. Increasingly, he sat in on political negotiations as part of Etienne's facilitation team. Rafael had come to enjoy those negotiations more and more. When the days were eighteen hours long and fraught with complex world issues there was no time to think about the things he'd said to Simone Duvalier.

And the things he hadn't.

Harrison had urged him to visit Caverness and speak with Simone in person. Harrison had urged that if returning to Caverness was the problem then perhaps Rafe could arrange to meet Simone in Paris instead. He'd urged Rafe to phone her, at the very least.

Rafael had picked up the phone and punched in the number for Caverness a hundred times over, but fear had stilled his hand. What could he offer Simone? Another night?

It wouldn't be enough for him.

Time shoehorned in between his commitments and hers?

His current commitments now spanned two countries and a small territory. Simone's covered all of Europe. Maybe if both parties were willing to juggle their schedules a little they might be able to manage a week here and there.

It still wouldn't be enough for him, but it'd be a start.

And then he would think back to those last raw words he'd thrown at her before she'd walked out of the

Sydney restaurant and knew himself a fool for thinking that Simone would ever want any kind of relationship with him at all after all he'd said and done.

She wouldn't.

All she would want was his apology. He owed her that much at the very least, and he should have made it weeks ago, months ago, for the longer he left it, the harder it got.

I'm sorry for the things I said.

That was the start of it. That was the easy bit.

If there was a woman in my life I could trust, I think it would be you.

If.

Was that an apology? He didn't know. He didn't think so.

The sun beat down on his back through the thin cotton of his shirt. Sweat slicked his skin from the effort of having taken to row upon row of hard and stony soil with a pickaxe. The gardeners had tried to stop him doing any of the physical restoration work when he'd first hoisted a shovel. Apparently princes of the realm did not labour like dogs beneath the fierce Maracey sun—even bastard ones.

They'd learned soon enough to leave this bastard alone when he was driving out his demons.

His mobile buzzed from amongst the assortment of tools in the wheelbarrow. Downing pickaxe, Rafe headed for it, his aching shoulders grateful for the reprieve, but as was the way of electronic devices, the buzzing had stopped by the time he reached it.

He wasn't in the mood to talk with anyone anyway.

Rafael reached for the water bottle he'd brought with him to the vines and opened it and quenched his thirst. Rosa the housekeeper would have a fit if she saw him.

Apparently bastard princes didn't fill up empty plastic water containers from the nearest tap, shove the bottle in the wheelbarrow, and drink it lukewarm as the impulse arose. Apparently they called the kitchen and left a request and someone brought a frosty glass of iced water out to him on a tray.

Rafe smirked briefly at the memory of Rosa explaining the procedure to him. He followed the memory with another long swig from the water bottle. He really wasn't that kind of prince.

The phone beeped again, short and sharp, signalling the presence of a message. Rafe capped the water bottle and put it down, picked the phone up and retrieved the message.

'Rafe, it's Gabrielle,' said the voice. 'I'm going to ring you again in two minutes' time and this time I expect you to answer your phone. I mean it, Rafael. You really shouldn't antagonise a woman in my condition. It's not good for the baby.'

Rafael grinned widely as he deleted the message. The phone rang again immediately. Same number. Impatient sister. This time he answered it. 'Congratulations.'

'Thank you,' she said magnanimously. 'Are you going to screen all your calls now you're a prince of the realm, or is it just the ones coming in from Caverness?'

'I'm well, thanks,' he said dryly. 'Kind of you to ask.'

'You even speak like a prince,' she muttered. 'Get out. Get out now.'

'When's your baby due?'

'In approximately seven months, two weeks and three days' time. Not that I'm counting.'

'I expect regular updates,' he said as he stared out over the wild Maracey valley. Gabrielle had warned him that there would be children. He was happy for her.

'How's the vineyard restoration going?' she said.

'The vineyard's a mess,' he said, looking around it.

'And the prince thing?'

'An even bigger ask.'

Gabrielle sighed. 'The thing is, when I look at you I can see why Etienne came for you. I *know* you can do the things he asks of you. So does Etienne, I suspect. The thing is, will you?'

'Is this a rhetorical question?'

'Possibly. But feel free to answer it anyway. I'm curious.'

'I don't know what I plan to do,' he admitted. 'I haven't made up my mind yet.'

'Are you happy there?'

He didn't know the answer to that question either. 'Sometimes.'

Gabrielle sighed again. 'Will you come and visit me soon?'

'Yes.' Finally a question that didn't require major contemplation.

'At Caverness?'

Rafael hesitated.

'Or if not Caverness, you could stay at Hammerschmidt. The vineyard restoration is coming together beautifully, and we're aiming to have most of the house restoration complete by the time the baby comes. Luc and I have decided to raise our family there. It's different now, Rafael,' said Gabrielle softly. 'Champagne. The village. Even Caverness. Just come. Come now.'

'Soon,' he countered. He knew it was time. Ready or not, he had to see Simone again and deliver his apology. 'How's Simone?' he asked gruffly.

'Rafe...' she said, and something in Gabrielle's

voice had every muscle in his body tensing. 'There's something I have to tell you. About Simone.'

'Is she ill?' he asked sharply.

'No. Not exactly. Rafe…' He could hear Gabrielle's struggle to find the right words. She *really* didn't want to deliver this news.

'Just say it,' he said.

'I'm not the only one who's expecting a baby around here, Rafael. Simone's pregnant too.'

The view shimmered before clicking back into focus. Once. Twice. Like reality gone wrong. 'Who's the father?'

'She doesn't say.'

The next question lodged in his throat, as if by holding it back he could put a brake on where his thoughts might take him, but they were already there and he had to know. 'When's it due?'

'Around the same date as mine. Rafael—'

'Stop,' he whispered.

'Rafael, I've never seen Simone so broken. She doesn't eat, she doesn't sleep, she doesn't even attend to her work. She just sits in the gardens of Caverness, and it's almost as if she doesn't even know that she's there. As if she's lost and can't find her way home.'

'Why are you telling me this?' He knew why. Heaven help him, he knew why.

'Because I love her. And because I think she loves you and is carrying your child and you don't even know it.'

Rafael closed his eyes and forced air into his lungs. He didn't know how much more he could take of this. Any of it.

'How does it feel, Rafael?' asked Gabrielle quietly. 'To walk in your father's shoes?'

CHAPTER SEVEN

RAFAEL stepped out of the car Etienne had loaned him and onto Champagne soil for the first time in nine long years. Caverness stood, as it had always stood, grey and forbidding, dominating the village below it as it had dominated him as a child. He'd sworn on his soul back then that he would never return to this place, but here he was and he could not regret it.

Some souls were more valuable than others.

He ran a hand through his hair, flexed his shoulders as if in preparation for battle, and headed for the kitchen door. He stopped abruptly, not knowing which door to use. Kitchen door or front door? Guest or family? Welcome or not?

He was spared further indecision when the kitchen door burst open and Gabrielle flew out, her face alight as she flung herself into his arms. 'You came,' she said as she covered his cheeks with kisses. 'I knew you would.'

Luc appeared in the doorway, his stance relaxed but his expression guarded. Gabrielle herded Rafe towards the door. Luc headed down the steps and started towards them. Rafael met his gaze warily. He knew this man like a brother. He knew exactly how fierce Lucien could be in defence of the people he loved.

'Gabrielle,' he muttered. 'Maybe you should go inside.'

'Have a little faith,' she whispered as she studied her husband. 'Luc sees both sides of this mess.'

'He has to do right by his sister. Honour demands it,' murmured Rafe as he set Gabrielle firmly behind him. He didn't think Gabrielle quite understood a brother's feelings towards a man who would take a woman to his bed for the night and then walk away without a backward glance. No matter what his reasons for doing so.

'If I didn't love you, I'd kill you,' said Luc simply as he stepped forward and drew Rafe into a fierce embrace. 'I still might.'

'You will not,' said Gabrielle sternly. And as Rafael stepped out of Luc's embrace, 'We've been waiting for you to arrive for two days. What took you so long?'

'I drove. I needed time to think.'

'Told you,' Luc said to his wife. 'Pay up.'

'Later,' said Gabrielle. 'You drove? You must be exhausted?' She eyed him critically. 'You are exhausted.'

'I'm fine.'

'Fatherhood's going to suit you,' murmured Luc.

'It will.' He exchanged another long glance with Luc.

'Told you,' Gabrielle said to her husband. 'Pay up.'

'Where is she?' said Rafael. Much as he wanted their company, he wanted Simone's more.

'In the old orchard garden,' said Gabrielle. 'Rafael?'

He'd already moved off. He stopped and forced his impatience into subservience as he turned back towards Gabrielle and Luc.

'I told her that I'd called you.'

'Fair enough.'

'She wasn't very happy with me.'

'I'll sort it out.'

'Well, yes. That's the plan. I'm hoping she'll forgive me eventually. Sisters should not fall out over men.'

'Fine,' he muttered, and started once more for the garden.

'Rafael?'

'What?' He stopped again, patience so clearly not one of his virtues that Luc started to laugh and Gabrielle rolled her eyes.

'I got you something to give to Simone. I didn't think you'd mind.' She speared him with a pointy finger and then pointed to the ground at his feet. 'Wait right there.' She disappeared back through the kitchen doorway and returned moments later with a small butter-coloured bundle in her arms.

Rafael looked closer.

The bundle had a nose. Two ears. Paws. Liquid brown eyes.

'It's a puppy,' he said stupidly.

'It's a golden retriever,' said Gabrielle as she bundled it into his arms. 'And it's a she.'

'She's fat,' he said next.

'Puppy fat,' said Gabrielle as she stroked the puppy's head. 'Don't you listen to him, sweetheart. You're not fat, you're Rubenesque, and you're going to grow up to be a rare beauty.'

The puppy squirmed in Rafael's arms. 'What is it you would have me *do* with this puppy?' he asked.

'You give it to Simone. As a gift.'

'Why?'

'Because.'

As far as reasoning went, it seemed a little…loose. 'Is this a pregnancy thing?' he said suspiciously.

'No, it's a *"you need something to help you even get a hearing"* thing,' said Gabrielle. 'Whatever it was you did to Simone, or said to her or *didn't* say to her, you hurt her, Rafael. Badly. You *need* to be part of a puppy package deal.'

'Are you sure about this?' He eyed the warm ball of puppyhood currently chewing on his watchband sceptically. Colour him practical, but he wasn't at all convinced that what Simone needed right now was a puppy. 'I really don't think you've thought this through.'

'Trust me,' said Gabrielle. 'Just do it.'

He found her in the old orchard, planting bulbs beneath an apple tree. She wore cut-off denim shorts, a pale pink T-shirt, a pair of old gardening gloves, and she'd pulled her silky black hair back into a loose ponytail at the base of her neck. Freshly pulled weeds sat in a pile on one side of her, fresh bulbs sat in a pile to the other side of her. He put the fat puppy down and watched in resignation as she headed straight for Simone and the bulbs and the dirt.

'Hello. Where did you come from?' Simone's voice came to him on the breeze, amused and welcoming. The puppy thought there was welcome in that voice too and, with her tail wagging furiously, she began to chew one of Simone's gardening gloves. Simone tapped the puppy lightly on the nose. 'And where are your manners?'

The Rubenesque puppy sat back, scratched its collar and promptly fell to chewing on the pile of weeds. Simone laughed and looked around, presumably for the puppy's owner.

And saw him.

Her laughter died as she scrambled to her feet and took the gloves off and brushed the dirt from her clothes. Apart from that first startled glance, she didn't look at him once.

'I like what you've done with the garden,' he said, by way of small talk. At this point, any type of talk would do, but Simone did not reply. Instead, she bent down and patted the puppy for at least half of eternity.

'What's her name?' she asked, after carefully checking the puppy's collar for a tag.

Name? What name? Pet *owners* decided on names. Not him.

'Or am I to assume that, like so many other animals in your possession, she simply doesn't have one?' said Simone.

'Ducks and swans do not need names,' he said a touch desperately. 'And this is…ah…' He watched in silence as the puppy abandoned its investigation of the weed pile in favour of digging in the dirt and retrieving some of the bulbs Simone had planted. What was he supposed to say? *Yours?* What on earth had his sister been *thinking*? 'Ruby,' he said. 'Ruby N Esquire.'

'How long have you had her?'

'Not long,' he said.

Simone stood up, shoving her hands in her back pockets as she did so. Her gaze held his for a moment before skittering away.

'I heard you were in Maracey,' she said quietly.

'I heard you were pregnant.' So much for small talk.

'Yes.' She lifted her chin, a tiny tilt of her head that he remembered of old, from the days when as a young girl she would square up and step up to take the blame for something that someone else had instigated. The children of Caverness protected their own. 'Yes, I am.'

'Is it mine?'

'It's a funny thing, the concept of ownership,' she said softly. 'I mean, we can care for things and tend things— I tend to this garden—but do we ever really own them?'

'Yes.' Rafael had *no* problem with the concept of ownership. 'Answer the question, Simone. Is this baby mine?'

'Given that hard-line ownership seems to be your thing, I'm going to start in the middle and call it ours.' She looked at him then and he saw it in her eyes already: a mother's protectiveness, fuelled in full by a mother's love. He wanted to weep.

He needed to apologise.

'Simone, those things I said to you at the hotel. I'm sorry. I was wrong and I knew it the moment I said them. I wanted to come after you. I wanted to talk to you about a million things. I wanted—' You. Just you. But the neediness of that statement made it too hard to voice. 'I wanted to come after you.'

'But you didn't.' She smiled tiredly and it struck him like a knife wound to his soul how fragile and defeated she looked. 'You never look back, Rafael. And sometimes…sometimes you should.'

'Come with me to Maracey,' he said desperately.

'Why?'

'So I can take care of you.'

'Look around you, Rafael. Am I short of money? In need of help?' She shook her head. 'If I need care, I can get it here. No. If you want me to accompany you to Maracey or Australia or wherever else you might end up, you'll need to offer me something else.'

'I'm offering to be a father to this child,' he said raggedly. 'Do you want marriage? Is that it?' He ran a hand around the back of his neck. 'I-I can do that too.'

'You just don't get it, do you?' she said quietly. 'Offer me something else.'

He would, but he had nothing else of any value to give. 'Would you like a puppy?'

She laughed at that, only it sounded more like a sob. 'Rafael, why are you here?'

'Because I have a responsibility to this baby and to you and I will *not* sit back and watch history repeat itself. I'm not like him, Simone. I'm not!'

Tears filled her beautiful brown eyes, but she blinked them back and looked away. 'I can't do this,' she whispered.

'Simone, please.' The puppy was back at his feet. He scooped it up and tucked it under one arm as he moved towards her, stopping just short of actually touching her, because if he did that he might never let her go. 'I'm trying to be what people want me to be and it's driving me mad. Nothing seems real any more. Not the past. Not the life I'm living in Maracey. Not the work that once consumed me.' He took a very deep breath. 'Not even this baby.'

She closed her eyes at that, shutting him out. 'My baby's real,' she whispered.

'Maybe to you. Please, Simone. I stood here before you years ago and offered you everything I had—all that I was—and it wasn't enough. It's still not enough—do you think I don't know that? But what else can I do?'

'Rafael, I—'

'Please.' There was no other way around this for him. 'Come with me to Maracey. We'll work something out. Just…come. Believe in me. Please. I won't let you down.'

He couldn't see it, she thought, and bled for him a little more. He couldn't see how many people already believed in him and loved him.

He thought he was alone.

'All right,' she said and patted the fat puppy in his arms and wondered why he'd called her Ruby, and lost her heart all over again as Rafael gently touched his fingers to her face and tucked a wayward strand of hair behind her ear. She took his hand and, with a tremulous smile, pressed her lips to his palm, before dropping his hand and stepping away, because if she touched him and held him, she might never let him go. 'Let me clean up here first.'

'And then?'

He stood there, an angel in her garden, so lost and wounded, so thoroughly prepared for rejection. How on earth could she ever convince such a scarred and weary warrior to lean on her, just a little, and maybe one day let her back in? 'And then I'll come with you to Maracey.'

CHAPTER EIGHT

RAFAEL brought the car to a smooth halt beside the tiny village parkland. Simone stifled a sigh. They'd spent the last two days on the road and the last two nights sleeping in farmhouse pensions, and, if Simone's Spanish sign reading served her correctly, they had just entered the territory of Maracey. Rather than push on to the vineyard estate, though, Rafael had stopped for a break.

In a moment the angelic-looking man occupying the driver's seat would turn towards her and ask her if she needed to stretch her legs or see to her toilette, or if she would like a drink or something to eat. He would look at her as if she were made of glass and she would glance down just to check that she wasn't, at which point she would look back up at him as if he'd gone mad.

Because, clearly, he had.

'Why have we stopped?' she asked sweetly. 'Again.'

'Puppy pit stop,' he said.

The puppy lay fast asleep at Simone's feet.

Rafael got out of the car and scanned his surroundings before leaning back down again to study her intently. 'Care for a walk? Drink? Something to eat?'

A kind woman would have said no, and that she was

just fine thank you because she'd walked, drunk and eaten less than two hours ago. A kind woman would have reassured him that pregnancy was a perfectly natural state for a woman and did not require such solicitousness on his part. Only a terrible woman would send the man off in search of some exotic juice that he'd never be able to find in a small village shop.

'I'm thinking kiwi-fruit juice,' she said airily.

'Kiwi-fruit juice.'

'Oh, yes. You see, kiwi fruit is green and green is good for the baby. I've been reading up on these things.'

'Right,' he said distractedly. 'Green.'

'And chicken.' Was it lunch time? Simone glanced at the dashboard clock. Close enough. 'I'd like some fried chicken too.'

'Right,' he said again and off he went. Man on a mission.

'Come on, Ruby,' Simone told the puppy as she nudged her awake and scooped her up. 'He wants us to walk.'

By the time Rafael returned some twenty minutes later, Simone and Ruby had done all the walking they intended to do and Simone had fished the picnic blanket from the car and spread it out beneath the dappled shade of an old oak tree. She'd just settled down on her back to partake of a tiny snooze when Rafael returned with lunch.

'Are you ill?' he said abruptly. 'How are you feeling?'

'Fine,' she said, sitting up and regarding him with no little exasperation, while Ruby greeted him ecstatically. 'I'm feeling fine. Blooming marvellous.'

Rafe's gaze sped to her stomach. Oh, yes. This baby business had messed with his mind, good and proper.

'I couldn't find any kiwi-fruit juice,' he said and

handed her a white polystyrene hot food container. Simone opened the lid, expecting chicken. She shut it again fast.

'I had them pick it and prepare it for you,' said Rafael.

She peeked again. 'What is it?'

'Boiled spinach.'

'Oh.'

'It's green,' he said helpfully.

'It certainly is.' And it served her right. She eyed the larger plastic bag he carried hopefully. Ruby eyed it too. 'Is there chicken?'

'Yes.' He studied her again, as if examining her for flaws. 'Gabrielle said you weren't eating properly.'

'Gabrielle exaggerates.'

'Or sleeping properly.'

That one was true. 'Let's just say that trying to figure out how and when to tell you about this baby was weighing on my mind. I know there are still a lot of decisions to be made about what we're going to do from here on in, but at least that bit's done.'

'So you've been sleeping a little easier?'

'A little.' No thanks to him. Rafael had slept in a separate room these past two nights, and kept physical contact with her to a minimum during the day. Neither action was particularly to her liking. She set the spinach aside and leaned back on her elbows as Rafael settled on the blanket beside her—not too close—and unpacked the shopping bag. Fried chicken, plain water, napkins, a kilo or ten of snow peas, and two green apples.

She shifted uncomfortably, turning her stomach towards him as she tilted over onto her side and smoothed the blanket beneath her, before settling back down.

'What is it?' he said in instant alarm.

'A stick digging into my backside.'

'Do you need a pillow?'

'Oh, for heaven's sake!' Simone yanked her T-shirt up to her midriff, grabbed Rafe's hand, and placed it palm down on her stomach. Maybe if he felt for himself, he wouldn't be so worried about this baby's current position in the world. 'You can't feel any movement yet,' she told him. 'It's too early for that, but this baby is well protected and healthy, Rafael, and so am I.' She stared up into those vivid blue eyes and offered him a smile. 'Can you feel it?'

'Feel what?' All Rafael could feel was skin, warm and silky. All he wanted was more. His body responded instantly, brutally focused on the one woman he had absolutely no notion of how to handle. What did she *want* from him?

And what dared he give?

'My body,' she said, as if he needed the reminder that his hand now caressed it. 'It's rounder. Fuller.'

He couldn't feel a difference.

'Lower,' she murmured and covered his hand with hers and slid his hand lower and lower still so that their fingers disappeared beneath the waistband of her loose cotton trousers. Her fingers slid away, leaving only his in place, and her gaze met his dark and knowing. 'Can you feel it now?'

He couldn't. He was too busy trying to stem the insatiable need erupting inside him.

'Lower,' she whispered and arched her lower body up into his hand. She smiled. It was not the smile of a Madonna with child.

Rafael cursed and snatched his hand away fast, and put some distance between them along with whatever objects came to hand. The chicken. A thousand snow peas. A roly-poly puppy.

'Oh, look,' she said, staring across the park towards a small hotel. 'A pension.'

'No,' he said gruffly.

'You don't want me?'

He did want her. Insanely. 'Are pregnant women always this forward?'

'Are fathers-to-be always this batty?' she countered. 'You got me pregnant the regular way, Rafael. I'm really not the fragile virgin Madonna type.'

'I noticed.'

'I'm so pleased,' she said, eyeing him darkly. 'And just for future reference, my sexual appetite hasn't dimmed with early pregnancy. If anything, it seems to have increased.' She sat up and eyed the basket of fried chicken. 'I just don't know *what* comes over me at times. Chicken wing?'

'No.' If his voice sounded a little hoarse there was good reason for it. Denying one's deepest instincts took effort.

'Oh, good,' she said, and picked up the wing and bit into it with every appearance of profound enjoyment.

Simone let the angelic man with the fire of retribution in his eyes be after that, and concentrated on eating a balanced meal. The chicken wing. A *little* of the spinach. The snow peas were sweet and crunchy, and a much nicer green. She ate a handful of those and settled back to quiz Rafe about his status in this land as he finished his meal.

'What exactly is it that Etienne expects of you?' she asked him.

'My presence at certain state functions. My presence, on occasion, at politically sensitive meetings.'

'And how does Etienne introduce you?'

'As his son.'

'Does he ask for your input?'

'Yes.'

'And do you give it?'

'Sometimes.'

Simone studied Rafael solemnly. Etienne asked a lot from his newfound son.

'Does he give you time to relax?'

'Overseeing the restoration of the vineyard is relaxing.'

'You've taken that on too? As well as running your own vineyard from afar?'

'I've put a manager in place at Angels Landing.' The grimness of Rafael's features told her just how much it had pained him to do so. More than any of the other projects surrounding him, Angels Landing was *his* dream, and he'd worked hard for it. It didn't seem right that he'd had to give it up to make room for other people's agendas.

'Is this manager any good?'

'Maintenance-wise, he's very thorough. Vision-wise, he still needs guidance, but Harrison's overseeing that at the moment. Harrison says he's doing all right.'

'Good.' Simone nodded and made a mental note of Rafael's reliance on Harrison's judgement. She made another note to ask Harrison to visit them in Maracey as soon as practicable. Rafael needed people he could trust around him. The list of people who'd earned such trust would not be a long one. 'Does Etienne reside at the vineyard estate?'

'No. He's based at a castle in the capital. There are rooms in the castle set aside for my use should I wish to stay there, apparently, but I prefer the vineyard. Whether I stay in Maracey at all is an issue currently up for debate amongst Etienne's senior statesmen.' Rafael's expression hardened. 'It seems not everyone is happy to see me.'

'Is that so?' Simone smiled tightly. She wondered if those statesmen knew how used to rejection this man was and how fiercely he'd learned to fight for the things he considered his. Heaven help them if he decided he wanted Maracey.

'You'll be staying with me at the vineyard,' said Rafael next. 'I've asked the staff to prepare a suite for you. Hopefully sleep will come even easier to you once you're settled there.'

'No.'

'Pardon?'

Simone sighed heavily. She'd tried showing him what she wanted from him, but to no avail. It was time to spell it out for him using words he could understand. The 'fragile virgin Madonna' treatment had to stop. She was not fragile, and she was certainly no virgin. She quite liked being thought of as a Madonna, but that was probably just the pregnancy talking. 'No. No separate suite, no separate bed. And no treating me like a stranger. I have a different proposal for you.'

'If you want me to marry you, I'll marry you,' he said curtly.

He would too. Simone sighed. For an intelligent man, he seemed exceptionally good at missing the point. 'Put your obligatory proposal and your narrow-eyed looks away,' she said evenly. 'I don't want to marry you. Marriage requires love and intimacy. Trust. And you and I… We don't have any of those things.' Yet. 'No, my proposal is designed to see us through our stay at Maracey, that's all.' And perhaps foster a few of those things that they didn't yet have.

'What did you have in mind?' he asked warily.

'A far less complicated merger,' she said carefully. 'You give me something that I want, and I'll give you something that you want.'

'What would you have of me?'

'A little of your time during each day.' She speared him with a glance. 'And your bed every night. I find I like it there.'

He absorbed her blunt words with considerable aplomb. He leaned back against the trunk of the tree, put his hand to his neck and rubbed. 'Well...' he said slowly. '*Some* of that sounds manageable.' His gaze didn't leave hers. 'What would you give me in return?'

'I know social politics, Rafael. I know the ruthless games of big business. I know them very well. I can be of use to you when it comes to Maracey and its nervous statesmen if you let me. I can watch your back on the rare occasion that you're not standing against the wall.'

He said nothing.

She didn't bother with telling him that she would do this for him whether he wanted her to or not and that she'd do it because she loved him. He wouldn't believe her. Eventually, though, he would have to believe in her love for him. The evidence would have it no other way. Then all she had to do was make him fall in love with her and everything would fall into place. This baby. This lifestyle, whatever it was...

Rome wasn't built in a day, she reminded herself by way of encouragement, and set about laying another brick. 'I didn't come all this way with you to be treated like a porcelain princess, Rafael. I swear I'll go nuts if you continue to treat me like one.'

'My mistake.' He smiled slightly, a tiny glimpse of sunshine on a cloudy day. 'What sort of princess would you like to be?'

She favoured him with a gentle smile. 'Yours.'

They arrived at the fortress just after four in the afternoon. The sun still burned high in the sky, but later it would disappear behind the hillside and shadows would creep over the valley. This was a place of sunrises, not sunsets. Of shimmering beginnings that stole slowly across the landscape before bathing a body in light.

Rafael hoped Simone would like it here. They'd discussed no long-term plans beyond her accompanying him to Maracey, the main reason for that being that he didn't currently *know* what the future would hold or whether he wanted to stay in Maracey permanently and become heir to the throne. Now Simone's thoughts and feelings would have to be added to the already complex mix.

At least she was here. That was the main thing. Here at his begging; he remembered that too. Not loving him, not wanting to marry him. Wanting only his bed.

Heaven help them both.

Rafael drove up to the outer entry gates, great wooden-beamed and steel-braced squares. They opened silently, electronically driven, and closed just as silently behind them. The inner walls had ramparts and walkways atop them. Rafael knew for a fact that when Etienne was in residence those walkways would come into use. Simone's eyes widened.

Okay, so there were one or two drawbacks to palatial living. But a person could forgive a lot when they woke to views over a valley that only soaring eagles shared.

'It's bleaker than I remembered,' she murmured.

Of course. She'd been here before as a child. 'It's not bleak inside,' he assured her and she slid him an assessing glance as he parked the car by the entrance portico and cut the engine.

'You *like* it here,' she accused mildly. 'The isolation, the fortress, the burning sun.'

'Maybe. I may have become somewhat addicted to watching the sun rise from that balcony right there,' he said, and pointed up to the patio jutting out from his bedroom.

Simone opened the car door and Ruby tumbled out. Simone followed more gracefully and looked up at the balcony before turning to regard the valley spread out before them. 'I can see why,' she said softly.

'Staff-wise, there's a head housekeeper who lives in and also cooks for whoever's in residence. There's day cleaning staff—three of them come every day and there are others on call. There's a head groundsman who also lives on the estate. He has staff as well. There's also a security contingent present,' he told her as the double entrance doors opened and the stern and angular Rosa stepped out to greet them. 'That's Rosa, Head Housekeeper. She speaks French, English, Spanish and the local dialect here, and she despairs of my lack of ceremony. Her day staff like her and she has a knack for getting good work out of them. She's proudly Maracenian and can be a bit haughty at times.' He stopped his assessment of Rosa at that. Simone was used to dealing with Josien, he reminded himself. Compared to Josien, Rosa was a sweetheart.

Rosa nodded and ushered them inside, out of the heat of the day. Rosa suggested refreshments in fifteen minutes, or as soon as they'd washed away their travels. Simone enthusiastically agreed.

Rosa attempted to show Simone to her suite.

Simone smiled and proceeded to tell the housekeeper to keep the suite they'd prepared for her
prepared by all means—for if she ever kicked Rafael
out of his bed he would need somewhere to sleep—but
that for now Simone was letting him sleep in his own
room with her and Ruby the fat puppy.

Rosa's stern features registered surprise, quickly
followed by a flash of what might have been approval.
Simone held the other woman's gaze and lifted an im-
perious eyebrow. Rosa bowed her head, but not before
Rafael saw the smile hovering about the housekeeper's
lips. It *was* approval.

Ruby chose that moment to be a puddly puppy and
anoint the glossy marble floor.

Rosa winced. Simone sighed.

'All right, point taken,' said Simone. 'The puppy can
sleep wherever it is fat puppies sleep around here. But
I'm standing firm on my own sleeping arrangements.
No guest suite.' She looked towards Rafe. 'I sleep with
him.'

Rafael relaxed in spite of himself and allowed himself a smile.

Both women stopped their discussion and stared.
Rosa in astonishment, Simone in wry acknowledgement.

'Did you see that?' whispered Rosa. 'Like sunshine.'

'You should have seen him as a child, back when responsibility didn't have quite the hold on him that it
does now,' murmured Simone. 'His smile could warm
a whole day.'

But Rafael's smile had dimmed at the reminder of
the responsibilities that he did now carry. 'Simone's
pregnant,' he told the housekeeper bluntly. 'Can you
adjust your menus accordingly?'

'Not that this pregnancy's been playing on his mind or anything,' added Simone. 'Much.'

The housekeeper eyed Simone's still svelte form. 'But of course we can alter the menus. There are foods she must have and foods she can't.'

'Easy on the can't,' murmured Simone. 'The minute you say I can't have something I tend to want it more.'

Rosa nodded sagely. 'Come to see me in the kitchen and we shall discuss preferences.' Rosa leaned closer to Simone. '*El ángel*, there, he has no preferences or favourites. I have a food budget that allows for the finest of ingredients and all he tells me is that he eats anything. Everything! Where's the challenge in that?'

'Inexcusable,' murmured Simone with a shake of her head. She was, after all, French. 'As for your impending fatherhood,' she added and speared him with a very direct glance, 'you really shouldn't go blurting it out like that. Does Etienne know?'

Er…

She read the answer on his face. 'While I am confident of Rosa's discretion, Rafael, there's *gossip*, and then there's gossip. May I borrow your phone?'

Wordlessly he handed it to her and watched as she scrolled through his contacts list until she found the number she wanted.

'Your Highness? It's Simone Duvalier. Yes, we've just arrived at your magnificent estate. Yes, such a beautiful drive and so relaxing. We stopped so many times along the way to take in the views.' Simone had dug a notepad from her handbag and was busy scribbling on it while his phone balanced precariously between cheek and lightly tanned shoulder. She held the note up for his and Rosa's viewing pleasure. It said, 'Dinner for three at eight?'

Rosa nodded vigorously.

Rafael shrugged indifferently. While he admired Etienne as a ruler, His Royal Highness had considerable shortcomings as a father. Etienne was trying, Rafael did give him that. But the father-son relationship that Etienne had been so intent on securing had far more to do with matters of state than it had to do with affection. Etienne would be thrilled by the notion of a new generation of little royal children who would, of course, be expected to fulfil their duty to Maracey and secure the royal line. Whether Etienne would ever be a *grandfather* to those children was open to speculation.

Children, he realised with a start. Not child. He wasn't thinking of just one, and that was the danger of having Simone by his side. He wanted this child, their child, with an intensity that left him breathless. He wanted more.

Simone, by her actions and demands, was making it crystal clear that she had no intention of being a burden to him. She was not disguising her strengths or the assets she could bring to his table. She was here to see if they could make a relationship between them work. A practical woman.

A remarkable one.

For the first time in ten weeks, Rafael felt a ray of hope touch him and find purchase in his soul. As if somehow, with Simone at his side, there might be a way of making all these newfound responsibilities mesh together.

'Etienne, would you like to join us here for dinner?' he heard her ask. 'Say, dinner to be served at eight? I'm pregnant, Rafe's the father, and we're celebrating.'

Rosa snorted. Simone grinned, and Rafael crossed his arms in front of him, eyebrow raised at her deliberately breezy delivery of such news. But he felt like smiling.

'You would?' she said next. 'Wonderful. But of course. *Adios. Bon soir.* Bye.'

Snapping the phone shut, Simone handed it back to him with a smile he knew of old. 'That ought to keep his senior statesmen spinning for a while. Rosa, you may now tell the world.'

Rosa smiled broadly. 'As the *mademoiselle* commands.'

Simone smiled back, every inch the wanton, wilful and *very* astute princess. 'You know what?' she said as she tucked her hand in the crook of his arm and looked curiously around the foyer. 'I think I'm going to like it here.'

Etienne arrived at exactly a quarter to eight that evening, and bearing two small gifts. A slim, leather-bound edition of poems that he handed to Rafael and a posy of violets that he bestowed on Simone.

Rafael looked at the violets and something turned inside him and clicked. He'd collected violets for Josien as a boy, searching valiantly for the first blooms of the season, those tiny fragrant petals that hid between fat green leaves. They'd always made Josien go quiet when he gave them to her. They always made her turn away.

Had Etienne given his mother violets once too? Had Josien once been deeply in love with the young prince Etienne?

'Love poems,' said Simone approvingly as she glanced at the book in Rafe's hands. 'Even Tennyson. Now there's a man who could have almost been French, such was his understanding of the heart.'

'There's a marriage proposal in there somewhere,' said Etienne. 'Should anyone ever need one.'

'Is there?' Simone bestowed a charming smile on

Etienne. A smile Rafael had learned a long time ago to be wary of. Etienne would learn Simone's ways soon enough. Etienne was a master at reading people, but for now Rafe stood back and prepared to enjoy the show as Simone and Etienne established the lay of the land when it came to poets and proposals.

'It's a modern world, Your Highness, with modern ways,' said Simone lightly. 'And while I can understand your interest in Rafael's intentions towards me, and mine towards him, let me be perfectly clear about something. I will have no interference or outside pressure brought to bear on our relationship.'

With a great deal of innate grace, Simone slid the book from Rafe's unprotesting hand and set it on the side table before turning back and bestowing yet another smile on Etienne, only this time she'd swapped charm for steel. 'I'm sure you of all people understand the need for any decision on marriage to be ours rather than one of necessities of State.'

'Well said,' added Rafe, bringing Etienne's appraising gaze around to rest on him. There were some things Rafael was willing to do for Maracey. And some things he would not. *Don't push me.* He held Etienne's gaze. *I'm here and I'm playing your stately games the way you want them played, but I guarantee you will not like the results when you push me.*

Noted, was Etienne's silent rejoinder as he turned back towards Simone, warier now, and well he should be. 'My son is a constant surprise to me.'

'Really?' Simone's expression softened as she looked at Rafael. 'How sad. But then, had you acknowledged him as a child, he wouldn't be the man he is today. And that would be a shame.'

'You never knew your mother, did you?' asked

Etienne. 'Such a beautiful woman and remarkably astute. Fiercely loyal to your father, of course. Every bit his equal and absolutely fearless in his defence. A valuable ally. A dangerous enemy. You remind me of her.'

'Thank you.' Simone's polite smile didn't waver. Rafael stepped closer to her, instinctively wanting to shield her from Etienne's remarks, no matter how innocuous they seemed on the surface. The children of Caverness protected their own and talk of mothers was not encouraged. 'I'll take that as a compliment.'

'You should,' said Etienne. 'I do hope we're not going to become enemies, *mademoiselle*.'

'So do I, Your Highness.' Simone favoured him with the sweetest of smiles. 'You used to call me Simone once.'

'You used to call me Etienne.'

'Shall we attempt it?' she said. 'For the sake of peace, prosperity, and the debt you owe your son and his unborn child?'

'That's quite a card you have to play,' said Etienne after a thoughtful pause.

'I know,' said Simone. 'Brilliant, isn't it? And I intend to keep playing it. Someone has to look out for Rafael's best interests. He's far too fond of putting other people's wants and needs ahead of his own. Not that he would ever admit it.' Another smile, impish this time and directed solely at Rafael. 'Is there a parapet we can go and stand on while we take our refreshments before dinner? I have this longing to be outside with the breeze on my skin and the sun at my back while I watch dusk fall over the valley below us. This is such a beautiful place, and it's such a glorious evening.'

It was, thought Rafael. It really was.

Harmony had been discussed, obtained, and now it ruled.

Diplomacy, Duvalier style.

Dinner went well. The food was excellent, the service unobtrusively stately, and the company extremely pleasant once the pesky issue of boundaries had been established. Etienne was a diplomat born and Simone had her own skills in that area, and together they worked on Rafael, drawing him out, drawing a smile every now and then, or a wickedly incisive take on issues Etienne had been dealing with. Rafe deliberately challenged Etienne at times, forcing the different point of view to be explored and defended. Usually, he did so without disclosing exactly where *his* views lay.

No wonder Etienne's elder statesmen were in a panic, thought Simone wryly. If they were smart they were beginning to realise Rafael's intelligence and the strength of his will. If they were smarter still they would be beginning to see that he had no intention of ever being their puppet. Did Etienne himself know the full potential of this son he'd finally claimed?

Watching and listening to them, Simone realised that he did. Etienne knew full well just how strong and smart a leader Rafael had the potential to be. Their relationship was a strange mixture of the formality of strangers coupled with a determination on Etienne's part to chip away at Rafael's barriers and an equally determined Rafael who kept taking Etienne's chisels away.

A father-son relationship between these two would take time, but they might get there eventually. Rafe's defences *were* down, never mind how expertly he hid that fact. Simone knew him too well. She knew the signs. Rafe had had one too many surprises. His life had undergone one too many changes and he hadn't re-grouped yet.

A clever father would take advantage of this tempo-rary doorway into the real Rafael.

A woman who loved him would take advantage of it too.

Simone walked with Rafael and Etienne to the door. She'd wondered about farewelling Etienne early and giving them this time alone, but Rafael must have sensed her intention and with a tiny shake of his head had indicated that there was no need.

Would a woman in love put her own need to be of use to her man ahead of her desire to see a father and son reconciled?

Damn right she would.

Etienne opened the front door and stepped outside and suddenly an entourage of dark-suited bodyguards appeared as if from nowhere. More dark-suited men pa-trolled the inner fortress wall. *More* dark-clothed men stood in the shadows of the outer fortress wall. Those ones hadn't moved at all.

'Were the security guards here when we arrived?' Simone asked Rafael as they watched Etienne and his entourage get under way and peel out of the fortress with military precision. She hadn't noticed any guards roaming the grounds earlier, but there were certainly still plenty in place now that Etienne had gone.

'Some were,' murmured Rafael. 'I spoke to the head of security here earlier. He arranged for more.'

'Because Etienne was visiting?'

'Because there's more to secure now that you're here.'

Simone instinctively put her hand to her stomach. 'Is there a threat I should know about?'

'No. Maracey takes the safety of its royal family

very seriously, that's all,' he told her. 'It's in the princess manual fine print.'

'What else is in the princess manual fine print?' asked Simone warily.

'Security cameras in every room, armoured cars, food tasters…'

'*What?*'

Rafael grinned. Simone took one look at him and thumped him on the arm.

'Okay, I may have been kidding about the food tasters,' he conceded.

'You'd better be kidding about the security cameras in every room as well.'

'How about I just tell you where they aren't?'

'How about you just *show* me where they aren't?'

Rafael grinned again and lit Simone's night. No doubt about it, she and the baby had been thrust upon him. But sometimes, with a smile or with a glance, she got the feeling that, thrust upon him or not, Rafael liked having her around.

With a passion.

A woman could build on that. A woman could hope.

'Rosa's prepared a bed for Ruby downstairs,' said Rafael. 'The head gardener seems quite taken with her. Says he'll check on her through the night and let her outside when need be.'

'Let's hope no one shoots her,' said Simone with a final glance at the men on the ramparts before stepping back inside.

'The guards all know she's here,' said Rafael. 'I'm more fearful for the head gardener's flowers,' said Rafael. They headed for the master suite in companionable silence. Once there, Simone eyed the ceilings and corners for security cameras.

'There's none in here,' murmured Rafael, watching her from the doorway.

Just as well.

Simone's belongings had been brought to the suite earlier and packed neatly away. She'd dressed for dinner in here, cluttering up the room as she went. Her handbag on the floor beside a dresser. A scarf flung over the back of a chair. It helped, she thought, that Rafael had not made the room his. It helped that they were both strangers to this space. She slid him a glance.

His stillness telegraphed volumes. He had not moved from his position beside the door, but he watched her every move. Gauging it. Waiting for her next move, if only she dared make it.

'I watched you tonight,' she said conversationally.

'I noticed.' He didn't smile, and that was a pity. 'What was the verdict?'

'That you would make a good ruler of Maracey one day. Should you choose to be. That we would make a politically powerful combination. Should we choose that path. And that, prince or not, you can still warm me with nothing more than a glance and a smile.' She reached for her hairpins and began to take down her hair. 'Should you choose to.'

She slipped off her shoes and slid them beneath the bed. 'I know I forced my company upon you here in this bedroom. I did it because I wanted to strengthen your position here, not weaken it by appearing to have been thrust upon you. I did it because I realised some time ago that one night in your bed simply wasn't enough for me. I want more. I want this relationship to be real.'

She looked around the sumptuous bedroom with its fabulous furnishings and the lake-sized bathroom branching off from it with its spectacular sunken spa. 'Okay, as real as it can be with you deciding whether you want to be a prince of the realm and me wondering what else is in the princess manual fine print that I'm really not ready for.'

'The security bothers you?' he asked quietly.

'A little. It points to a potential lack of privacy that could bother me a lot.'

'I'll do everything I can to ensure that the privacy versus protection balance works for you.'

'For us,' she corrected gently. 'And thank you. I do however realise that it's part of the royal family package and might not be something either of us have a lot of control over. But that's really not the point I was trying to make.'

'It's not?'

'No. I just got sidetracked by that one for a moment. I'm pretty sure I was trying to make a different point altogether. It was about our expectations of one another here in this bedroom.'

Clarity was a must.

Confidence was vital.

There could be no weakness in her approach to sharing Rafael's bed. She wanted to. Very much. But he had to want it too. 'I want to make love with you again, Rafael. I would like it to be an ongoing arrangement. The thing is, my feelings aren't the only feelings that need to be considered. Yours do too so I'm asking you plainly.' The last hairpin came out. She placed them on the dresser and shook out her hair. 'What would you have from me here in this bedroom?'

'What would you give?' he asked huskily.

She gave his question the thought it deserved. 'Anything.'

'Anything?' He made the word a caress, full of dark needs and wicked promise.

'Anything you asked for.' She knew this man. She knew his soul. Fierce but not cruel. Wild but not destructive. Intensely protective of those few things that he loved beyond measure. She wasn't one of them, she knew that. But she did not doubt that whatever he demanded of her, he would keep her safe. 'So ask.'

His eyes grew dark. She was trying to make this simple for him. Whatever he wanted, be it separate sides of the bed or an arrangement with a little more fire to it, all he had to do was ask. She didn't think asking a man to state what he wanted was too torturous a question.

Then again, this *was* Rafael.

'Come here,' he murmured.

She went to him. Stood in front of him, not touching him, not yet. 'What else would you have?'

His smile came slow and sure. He liked this game. Damned if he didn't. 'Put your hands on me,' he said next.

'Where?'

'Anywhere.'

'I want them on skin,' she murmured.

He shed his shirt and stared at her in silent challenge, all washboard hard and hungry male as the balance of power shifted and shifted again.

Choices, choices.

She placed her hand on the plane of his stomach. He shuddered beneath her touch and his eyes grew heavy-lidded.

'More,' he murmured.

She put her other hand on his arm, just above his elbow, and slid it up to his shoulder. Plenty of hills and valleys worthy of exploration there. 'What else would you have?' she murmured.

'More.'

'Could you be a little more specific?' She raked her nails lightly down his chest. Rafe's breath left his body with a hiss.

'Lose the clothes, Simone, forget the game, and stand naked before me.'

He asked a lot, this man, but she did it because he needed her to and because she would demand no less from him before this night was through. 'What now?' She shivered, just a little, in the cool night air. Her nipples tightened and she lifted her chin to show that she was not afraid, no matter what he asked of her.

He smiled at that, slow and wicked. 'Cold?'

Not any more.

'Come closer.' Another order and one she obeyed. She was rewarded with a kiss, deep and drugging. 'Tell me when to stop,' he muttered. 'The baby…'

'The baby is fine,' she whispered, and arched into his hands as he grazed the curve of her neck with his teeth. 'And hell will freeze over before I ever tell you to stop.'

He needed this, thought Rafael. The protection Simone afforded him so effortlessly. The passion she offered so willingly. And the trust she placed in him. 'It's not a fair bargain,' he murmured and he nipped at her shoulder blade and trailed his fingers down her spine. 'This proposal of yours, I see nothing in it for you.'

'That's because you're not looking through my eyes,' she murmured, and slanted him a glance as she undid his belt and the button on his trousers. 'I see plenty in this for me. Just…' Simone found him and caressed him, a slow slide of her palm against straining hardness and heated skin. His heartbeat tripled. 'Plenty.'

Rafael took her mouth again, an erotic tangle of lips and of tongues. The bed was here somewhere, he needed a bed, needed to be careful of this woman with his child in her womb. The need to protect warred with his need to possess. He could not predict which need would triumph.

He picked her up and carried her to the bed, laying her on her back before sinking down beside her. He ran his hand down her body, from shoulder to stomach and back to a tightly budded breast. Rafe bent his head and suckled hard. Simone gasped and bucked beneath his ministrations.

'Sensitive?' he whispered as her fingers came up to cradle his head.

'You have no idea.'

'More?'

'Yes,' she muttered and cried out her pleasure when he took to her other breast with a gentle scrape of teeth and tongue. Her hands were not gentle in his hair as she writhed beneath him. 'God, yes.'

To protect or to possess? Which would it be? Simone parted her legs willingly, wantonly, as he trailed kisses down her ribcage and over her gently rounded stomach.

'Would you like me to say your name?' she offered raggedly.

Possession won.

CHAPTER NINE

ONE week slipped by and then another as Simone settled into the rhythms of Maracey, its politics and its people. During the day Rafael belonged to Maracey and to Etienne, or that was the way it seemed. He did what Etienne asked of him and attended all manner of meetings, emerging from them preoccupied and remote, with his defences so solidly in place there was no getting round them. Only at night when reckless, insatiable passion ruled them both did Rafael become truly hers, taking everything she offered, and giving everything a woman could ever want in return.

Tenderness.

And surrender.

Passion.

And possession.

Whether love grew in such conditions, Simone could not say. Rafael never spoke of love and he never spoke of their future. She didn't know how long their stay in Maracey would last or whether Rafael intended to take on the role of Etienne's heir apparent. He was being groomed for it, that much was certain.

So many questions in need of answers.

Such a fragile thing, Rafael's trust in her.

Simone was three months pregnant now and her morning queasiness had become more pronounced. Rafe had taken to waking before her in the mornings and padding downstairs to the kitchen to collect whatever Rosa happened to be trialling that day that might, at a pinch, stay in her stomach for more than a minute. Fatty foods would not. Nor eggs, toast, fruit, yoghurt, cereal, croissants or baguettes. Day-old flat-bread would. Salted crispbread would too, washed down with unsweetened tea. Once she'd lined her stomach with food the morning sickness would pass. Until she was up and about though, Rafael hovered.

It helped immensely that he chose to do so in a pair of long cotton pyjama bottoms and nothing else. She loved watching him pace around as he lingered over his own breakfast, with one eye on getting ready to go do business and one on her. She loved that she could admire the craftsmanship on his back now without wincing.

Admittedly, that didn't stop her from suggesting a few minor improvements to the wording.

'You know, I *think*,' she said with a wave of her salted crispbread as he wandered past the bed for the umpteenth time, 'that with a tiny bit of finessing, a master artist could make that tattoo read "Honey, I'm Back".'

'No.' He continued on his way to wherever it was he was going. But his lips twitched and that was all the en-couragement she needed.

'"Wrong Way Go Back?"' she suggested next. 'Just in case you ever need to double as a roadside stop sign?'

He gave her a look that would have turned bacon crispy—had there actually been any bacon on her plate.

'You're right,' she said. 'It'd never work for women

drivers. They'd like as not drive off a cliff while looking at you. What about a nice solid square and no words at all. "Back in Black". Get it?'

His lips twitched. Possibly in humour. Possibly in pain. 'Eat your cracker,' he said.

She nibbled the salty bits off it thoughtfully. 'I've got it,' she said. '"The Love Shack."'

'The wording stays as is,' he said firmly. 'Get used to it.'

She *was* used to it. It was the pain beneath the words that she objected to, and she still didn't have the faintest idea how to make it go away. It was always there, in the emotional distance he demanded of others, in the way he kept his feelings to himself. 'I bet you can't wait for me to start suggesting names for this baby,' she said sagely.

'God help us,' he muttered.

'Well, she *could*. But you do realise she's going to push for one of those archangel names. Not that it isn't already a family theme. How about Michael?'

'Michael is good.'

'Uriel?'

The look he sent her indicated possibly not.

'Metatron! Now there's a goodie.'

'No,' he said sternly.

But he went to his meeting that day with a smile on his face.

Rafael lived to get through each day as best he could. He did what Etienne wanted and attended his meetings and sat through endless negotiations that had ramifications far beyond what he was used to thinking about. His respect for Etienne grew with each passing day. His feeling of entrapment grew with each passing day as well. Only the nights gave him solace. Only in Simone's arms did Rafael find freedom of a sort, and even that was weighted against the guilt of having forced Simone to accompany him to Maracey and into a lifestyle she did not want and made no comment on although he could see for himself the unhappiness in her eyes at times.

She was over three months pregnant now, and Rafael could detect the tiny changes in Simone's body almost as well as she could. He knew when morning sickness plagued her. He knew those rare days when it didn't. He loved those mornings when she lounged in bed and watched him dress, every inch the pampered and teasing princess.

This wasn't one of those mornings.

This morning Simone had shadows in her eyes as well as beneath them and he shifted restlessly beneath her solemn gaze.

'Rafael?' she said. 'May I ask you a question?'

'Of course.' He needed a suit for the day, dozens of which had miraculously appeared in the walk-in closet. He chose a grey one.

'Where are we going with this?'

'With what?'

'This relationship. Yours and mine.'

His hand stilled. He forced himself to breathe. 'I don't know.'

'We could discuss it?' she offered tentatively. 'Where we might go from here?'

'What's to discuss?' said Rafe as panic speared through him along with bone-jarring fear at the thought of having to watch her walk away from him yet again. Not yet. Not now. His need over hers and even as he thought it, even as he acknowledged his weakness and the depth of his need for this woman, he knew that he could not hold Simone here much longer if she truly wanted to leave. 'Do you want to leave me?'

'No.' She was by his side, taking his arm and turning him towards her. 'Rafael, no! I just want to know what your feelings are for this place and this lifestyle and for me. You never say,' she said in a small voice. 'You never say what *you* want.'

'I want to do right by you.' With all that he was. 'And the baby. I want you to be happy.' He gathered up his courage and bared his soul. 'With me.'

Simone's eyes filled with tears and she whirled away as quickly as she'd arrived. 'I hate her,' she said fiercely.

'Hate who?'

'Your mother.'

'I'm not overly fond of her myself,' murmured Rafael. He didn't quite see the connection between his statement of wants and Simone's statement of hate. 'So what?'

'So I need to think that one day you might trust me again. To stand by you. Not to hurt you. And I don't know if you ever will, because of your mother and the things she's done.' Simone crossed her arms around her body and hugged tight. 'And because of me and the things I've done and the situation we're in. And I need you to trust me, Rafael. This relationship won't work properly until you do.'

'Simone…' He didn't know what to say. 'I'm trying.'

She bowed her head. He couldn't see her tears, but her voice was thick with them. 'I know.'

Simone didn't see much of Rafael in the days that followed. For him it was meeting upon meeting, each one more important than the last. Each night saw him weary. Not weary of lovemaking, but weary of spirit and wary of everyone. Including her.

How much longer could he go on without letting anyone in?

She'd suggested they ask Harrison to visit Maracey and stay with them a while. She'd suggested they ask Luc and Gabrielle to visit them as well. Rafael needed people around him who he could trust and if not her then someone else. Negotiations on exactly what Rafael's role here in Maracey would involve were coming to a close. The stakes were high. The power Rafe wielded was already considerable.

Whether he *wanted* to wield it was anyone's guess.

Simone had taken to spending some of each lonely day in the old vineyard with Ruby the inquisitive puppy, a gardener's wheelbarrow, secateurs and gloves. The gardens immediately surrounding the fortress were fully formed and immaculately maintained, but here amongst the vines there was work still to be done and vision to be applied. Some of that vision, Simone had decided, would be hers.

The row of vines she worked her way along today had come from Caverness some thirty years ago. Her father had sent them and Etienne had planted them. Simone smirked as she straightened from her pruning and glanced down the row. Not that he'd planted them straight.

Still, they were a connection with her home, and one that she would see revived. She missed Caverness, there was no denying it. She missed the duties she'd borne within the Duvalier champagne empire and the people she'd worked with. She missed Lucien and Gabrielle and her favourite café. She missed being able to move freely through the outside world. To go where she pleased, whenever she pleased, and by whatever method of transport she pleased.

If Maracey had an outside world, she hadn't found it yet.

If there was freedom to be had here, she hadn't found that either. The high, cloister-like hedging around the terraced vines mirrored her sense of imprisonment but at least there was sky up above and a view down the valley that could make a spirit soar.

Rafael didn't even get that much, these days.

Simone pruned a wayward offshoot and tossed it towards the wheelbarrow. Much to Ruby's delight, it missed. Simone was trying to teach Ruby to retrieve the ill-aimed vines and drop them into the wheelbarrow, but Ruby had proven remarkably resistant to the idea. All retrieved vines, sticks and other assorted garden oddments would be dropped at Simone's feet in the hope that they would be thrown again and that was all there was to it.

Leaves rustled in the hedge behind her. Leaves did that occasionally, usually in response to a playful wind.

There was no wind.

Simone stared hard at the rambling hedge. It too was in need of a prune, albeit with a chainsaw rather than secateurs. Ruby took no notice of the hedge at all. Ruby the retriever had a likeable focus. Ruby retrieved.

Simone went back to her pruning.

'Look.' The whisper came to her on the wind, fairy light and childish. 'It's the princess.'

'Princesses don't prune grapes,' murmured another youthful voice, although the timbre of this one was male.

'Yes, they *do*.'

'Anyway,' said the boy voice, 'Mama says she's not

a princess until she marries the prince, and *he's* not a proper prince until the king says so.'

'It's still *her*,' said the little girl fairy.

Good point, thought Simone. No arguing with that. Excellent female logic. The girl fairy had potential.

'Move over a bit.' Leaves rustled. Ruby's ears pricked but her gaze stayed firmly fixed on the cutting in Simone's hand. Not exactly guard dog of the century, this one.

'Shh! You're making too much noise,' scolded the little girl fairy. 'She'll see us.'

Another good point, thought Simone. But boys would be boys. The leaves parted. Two childish faces peered out. Dark-haired, dark curious eyes, sunkissed Spanish complexions.

Simone raised her eyebrow and peered back at them.

The boy grinned, and something in his smile reminded her of another boy, long ago, and another bright and sunny day.

'Run, Melie, run. Race you to the gate,' he whispered, and then the leaves closed and they were gone.

Run.

How many times had she heard those words in her childhood?

Race you.

To gates and hills and castle walls, and through the vines. Memories crashed over her, vibrant and alive, as she hurtled back in time to another group of mischievous children, playing in the shadows of castle walls. If they weren't running from trouble there would be talk first, negotiation over head starts and what the losers would forfeit to the winner if they lost.

She'd always known that when Rafael started betting ridiculous cleaning chores like 'scrub the portrait room floor' or 'clean every window in the conservatory', it meant that Gabrielle had fallen foul of her mother and had been given that very chore to do. Rafe had always lost those races and picked up the chores. One single silent glance from Rafe had ensured that Simone and Luc had lost those races too.

The children of Caverness protected their own.

Somewhere along the way they'd all grown up, but some habits were hard to kick.

Simone was doing all she could to help Rafael adjust to this new life in Maracey. She feared it wasn't enough.

If he would only *trust* her a little more with his thoughts and his feelings.

But he didn't.

Tears burned her eyes and she blinked them away. Damn pregnancy hormones turning her emotions upside down. Amused one moment and tearful the next. Was there no escaping them? But there was no escaping the despair that came over her when she thought of her love for Rafael and of his continued distance from her. Not physically, not any more, but mentally, in a hundred tiny telltale ways. Maybe another woman would have been thrilled by what he did offer by way of companionship but Simone knew what he could offer, and what he *had* offered her all those years ago, and this wasn't it.

Maybe when the baby came things would improve. Maybe some of Rafael's love for his child would spill over onto her.

It wouldn't be enough.

'Go away, despair,' she muttered, helpless in its grasp and wanting it gone.

But just like Simone, it had nowhere to go.

Simone looked to the sky, she looked to the sun. Such a fierce, relentless fire, this Spanish sun. The secateurs slipped from her fingers as the sun swayed and the earth moved beneath her feet. Ruby moved too and picked up the secateurs. This time she dropped them in the wheelbarrow.

'Good girl,' whispered Simone and leaned down to pat her. The earth tilted alarmingly once more. This didn't feel right at all. The poky puppy smiled at her and tilted her head to one side and regarded Simone curiously. Just before everything went black.

Rafael watched with idle curiosity as Etienne's senior aide slipped into the meeting room as unobtrusively as possible. Given the delicacy of the water negotiations currently on the table, that wasn't very unobtrusively at all. Conversation ceased. The senior aide grimaced. Etienne scowled.

Whatever it was, thought Rafe, it had better be important.

But the aide did not cross to Etienne's side.

The aide came straight to him.

'*Señor,*' muttered the man as he bent down closer to Rafael's ear. 'It's your…it's the Señorita Simone. One of the guards found her in the vineyard. She'd been working there, tending the vines. *Señor*, we do not know what happened exactly but she's unconscious.'

Rafael stood abruptly. The aide moved back. Every gaze fixed on him. Some in censure, others with curiosity. He realised, as he'd been realising all morning, that diplomacy required a patience and a moral fluidity that he did not have. 'Gentlemen,' he said with a nod. 'Excuse me.'

Etienne would broker this deal, not Rafael.

Rafael Alexander belonged elsewhere.

He left without a backward glance.

Etienne called Carlos, his senior aide, to his side with a glance. Negotiations had been stalling all morning. Two of the three parties at the table were not ready for this discussion; they were simply biding their time and wasting his. 'Problem?' he murmured. *Tell me what you said to my son was what he meant. Tell me what you said to my wary and unapproachable son that had his face turning ashen and his eyes bleak with pain.*

'Señorita Simone fell unconscious in the vineyard,' murmured Carlos. 'El doctor's with her now.'

'And the baby?'

'I don't know.'

It had been years since Etienne's late wife had miscarried her babies, but a man did not forget such times or the bereavement and loss of faith in the goodness of life that invariably followed. Would Rafael want him there if Simone had lost the baby? Would this son who so baffled him want Etienne beside him on his bedside vigil or would he stand alone as he always seemed to do?

There was only one way to find out.

Etienne rose. So did everybody else. 'Gentlemen, a family matter needs my attention. I suggest we break for the rest of the day and reconvene tomorrow. You may be ready to sit at this table and negotiate by then. You may not. Give it some thought.' Carlos stared at him in horrified amazement, and well he should given that Etienne had just broken every unwritten rule of a peace broker's code of conduct. *He* was the one who was supposed to display patience when everyone around him had abandoned theirs. *He* was the one who was supposed to counsel continued negotiation in the often futile hope that something good would come of it.

He didn't.

He headed for the door, his aide at his heels. 'See if you can stop Rafael before he reaches his car,' he said to Carlos. 'Offer him the use of the helicopter.'

'The pilot's not here, Your Highness. Who's going to fly it?'

Etienne smiled grimly. Finally some small way in which he might be of use to his son. 'Me.'

Rafael paced the outer sitting room of the suite he shared with Simone. Etienne de Morsay, King of Maracey, negotiator extraordinaire, and—lately—helicopter pilot, sat on a nearby settee and waited with him, a silent, watchful presence. Rafael didn't know why Etienne had accompanied him. Maybe they were supposed to bond or something.

They didn't.

'Would you like me to call Harrison for you?' asked Etienne. 'I could arrange to get him here as soon as possible.'

'No.'

'Your sister, then?'

'No.'

'Someone else?'

'No,' he said tightly. 'I just want to see Simone.' The doctor had been in with her for ever. Rafael ran a hand through his hair and kept right on pacing. 'What's taking him so *long*?'

'The doctor is very good and very thorough. He's simply doing his job.'

Rafael scowled. 'Better that he did his job faster,' he muttered.

'Better he does it *well*,' corrected Etienne.

'Don't you have a meeting to attend to?' enquired Rafael sourly.

'No.'

The doctor emerged from the master bedroom, the door clicking closed behind him. Rafael stopped pacing abruptly. Etienne stood.

'What's wrong with her?' asked Rafael.

'As far as I can tell, nothing more than exhaustion and a touch of heatstroke. I've taken some blood samples to send for testing—the results will be back within a few days.'

'And the baby?' said Rafael.

'The baby's heartbeat is strong and there is no bleeding. I believe the baby will be fine provided the *señorita* rests for a day or two.' The doctor frowned. 'The *señorita*'s mind is fevered. I've given her something to help bring her temperature down, but right now she dreams uneasy dreams. She's protecting someone. A boy. A youth. She protects him in her sleep.'

Rafael cursed viciously.

'It will pass,' said the doctor gently.

Rafe said nothing, but he knew differently. They weren't dreams but memories. And no matter how hard a body tried to deny them they never went away.

Etienne thanked the doctor and saw him to the door.

Rafe slumped to a chair with the heels of his hands to his eyes. 'She dreams of me,' he muttered. 'She dreams of Caverness.' He passed his hands across his face. 'She guarded me then as she protects me now against foes both real and imaginary, and she shouldn't have to. I should be the one protecting *her*.'

Etienne said nothing.

Rafe sat forward, with his elbows on his knees and

his hands clasped before him. 'I'm ready to tell you what I want,' he told the older man, the one with eyes the same as his. 'What I'm willing to do for you and for Maracey.'

Etienne stared at him hard. 'You want to discuss this *now*?'

'Yes.'

'And will it be what you want or what you think the mother of your child needs?'

'It's the same thing,' said Rafe simply. 'I won't be staying in Maracey much longer. Not permanently. I'm not the son you're looking for.'

'You're wrong,' said Etienne. 'You're more than I ever hoped for.'

He couldn't have hoped for much, thought Rafe. 'From now on, Simone and I will be spending three months of every year at Angels Landing, and three months at Caverness,' he said as the idea unfurled before him. Caverness was Simone's home, Angels Landing was his. It seemed only fair. He thought Simone would think it fair. 'I want the Maracey vineyard estate deeded to my children and in return I will give you six months of my time every year. During that time I'll endeavour to learn as much as I can of matters of state. Give me ten years of this arrangement and I'll stand as your heir.'

'Done,' said Etienne simply.

So much for negotiation.

But there was one more point he had to make perfectly clear. 'Know this though. I will *never* put my responsibility towards this kingdom before my responsibility to Simone and my children. I'm not like you.'

'I'm glad,' said Etienne quietly. 'I'm glad that such a love sustains you.'

Rafe looked to his father and for the first time glimpsed the loneliness of the man who sat so seemingly effortlessly on the throne of Maracey.

'My choices haven't always been the right choices, Rafael,' said Etienne softly. 'Particularly where you and your mother were concerned. We both know that. But they were the only ones I felt I could make at the time.'

Etienne offered no other excuses, no explanation beyond those few words, but Rafe had picked up bits and pieces of the story from the papers and from the king's aides. How Etienne's parents had perished in a light plane crash. How the young prince, fresh from his studies in France, had returned from his stay in Champagne, picked up his father's mantle and been married within weeks to the considerably older and politically astute Mariette Sulemon. A strategic union and by all accounts a happy one, aside from the fact that no children had ever come of it.

When had Etienne learned of Josien's pregnancy? wondered Rafael. Before his marriage or afterwards? Josien was the most secretive and aloof person he knew—apart from himself, he conceded wryly. Had Josien even *told* him she was carrying his child?

Rafe stood and headed for the door to the bedroom. He had to see Simone for himself, he wanted to try and ease her sleep, but after that... Rafael stopped and slowly turned back. He never looked back, but this time he did. A remarkable woman had once told him that sometimes he should. 'Will you wait for me? I don't know how long I'll be.'

'I'll wait,' said Etienne.

'I'd like to talk to you afterwards.'

'About what?' Etienne's eyes were piercingly familiar. 'Haven't we just reorganised the world?' His faint smile was familiar too.

'No, just the future.' Rafael took a deep breath. It was time. Past time. 'I want you to tell me about Josien.'

Simone woke to find herself in a dusk-lit room with a breeze blowing softly into it through a doorway to a balcony beyond. She didn't remember how she'd got here. The last thing she remembered was a fiery Spanish sun and a poky little puppy.

She put her hand to her head where a headache pounded away, throbbing and insistent. The movement caused more movement from somewhere just outside her peripheral vision. Her vision wasn't the greatest at the moment. Too many black dots, not enough sharp edges. Then Rafael came into view as he sat on the edge of the bed. Face of an angel. Soul of a warrior. Heart that didn't belong to her.

Now she remembered where she was.

'Hey,' she said by way of greeting.

'Hey, yourself.' His eyes were relieved. Far too searching for her liking. 'How are you feeling?'

She'd certainly felt better. 'So-so. What happened?'

'You fainted in the garden. You have a touch of sunstroke. And the baby's fine.'

Good news, then, apart from the fainting and the sunstroke part. She felt as if she'd slept the day away. A quick glance at the clock revealed that she probably had. Unless she'd slept for days, plural. 'It's still Friday, isn't it?'

A smile tugged at his lip. 'Yes.'

'So...what else has been happening while I was away?'

'Plenty.'

'Anything that should concern me?'

'Nothing that should concern you *now*. The doctor has seen you. He took some blood, and he gave you something to bring your temperature down. He wants you to rest. *I* want you to rest. And as soon as you have, I'm taking you back to Caverness.'

'What?' Her mind went as fuzzy as her vision. '*Why?* What happened? Did Etienne's dissident statesman finally win him over?'

'No. Nothing like that. Etienne's been waiting out there in the sitting room, worrying right along with me about whether you would be fine.' Rafael smiled briefly. 'The doctor says you need to rest, that's all, and I know you, Simone. You won't do that here.'

'I won't?' She didn't think she'd been doing too badly on that front. 'Why not?'

'Because you'll be too busy playing politics and trying to protect *me*.'

'Well…yes. That's part of the deal. It comes with the chef, the housekeeper, the cleaning staff, the cars, the castles and the princess dresses. I really don't think it's too big an ask.'

'I do,' he said. 'You're going home.'

'I am?' Simone closed her eyes before they started watering again. She wanted to go home, she realised. Even if only for a little while. She hadn't said goodbye to Caverness yet. Not properly. Maybe she never really would. But the thought of being away from Rafael made her head ache more than it already did. The knowledge that he wanted to send her away crushed her.

'And you?' she said faintly. She opened her eyes and saw by the look in his eyes and the strain on his face that Rafe had made a decision on his own future too. Rafael never made decisions lightly, but once he'd made them there was very little that could sway him. Love could. And duty too. But not much else. 'What will you do?'

'I thought…' He looked away. He swallowed hard. 'I want to go home too.'

'To Angels Landing?' she whispered.

'No.' It was costing him, this decision of his. It was costing him plenty. Simone stared hard at him, willing the dots and the fuzziness away as she waited for a reply that seemed an agonisingly long time coming. 'To Caverness.'

Simone heartily approved of Rafael's full plan for their future when finally he thought to reveal it to her, some two mornings after she'd first fainted. Whether he thought she would faint once more upon hearing it was anyone's guess, but she did not and Rafael's eyes lightened as she expressed her enthusiasm for the idea.

'You hear that, Ruby?' said Simone from her position propped against the bed head with everyone's pillows, including Rafael's, at her back. Ruby was currently under the bed somewhere and Simone was well aware that one of her slippers had disappeared under there with the still Rubenesque puppy. The minute Simone had lined her stomach she intended to retrieve that slipper. Or more accurately, what would be left of it. 'You're going to be an international jet-set puppy.'

Ruby did not reply. Probably just as well.

'She'll not be able to come to Australia with us,' warned Rafael. 'The quarantine period's too long.'

'A European jet-set puppy then. She can stay with Luc and Gabrielle when we go to Australia,' amended Simone. 'When do we leave?'

Rafael paced the room in his pyjama bottoms, the

soft glow of morning light making him appear more angelic than ever. 'I thought tomorrow. Etienne agreed. He's put Carlos to work planning a formal dinner at the castle tonight in our honour. I told him I'd let him know if you were well enough to attend.'

'And have you let him know that I'm well enough to attend?' she asked curiously.

'Are you?' he countered.

'Just checking how autocratic you're planning to get,' she said airily. 'Of course I'm well enough to attend. Thank you for asking.'

'You're welcome.' His lips twitched. His eyes stayed sombre. 'I set this course for us just after you collapsed.'

'I fainted,' she said firmly. 'I did not collapse.'

Rafael ignored her massaging of the facts. 'I was waiting for the doctor to finish examining you. Etienne agreed to it.'

'Did he have a choice?'

Another faint smile. 'No. But you do. If you'd rather we made different plans, just say so.'

'I like this course you've set,' she assured him gently. 'A princess for six months, a champagne heiress for three more, and a winemaker's muse for the final three months of every year. I could embrace them all. Turn around.'

He turned towards her.

'No, the other around.' The one where his back was towards her.

He didn't oblige. He knew now, from experience, that looking would be followed by touching and that touching invariably led to lovemaking. He'd been extremely careful to limit her touching these past two days. Doctor's orders.

'I'm having a thought,' she said.

'If it involves rewording the artwork, the answer's no.'

'It's a really good thought.'

'No. Eat your flatbread.'

'I think I'm over flatbread for breakfast,' she said with a delicate shudder. Rafe eyed her warily, probably wondering whether a dash to the bathroom was in the offing. It wasn't. Playing with the delectable vision of angel-faced and wickedly built masculinity before her was.

'I'm thinking that if it's a girl we should abandon the archangel names altogether. Metatronella's really not working for me.'

'Couldn't agree more,' he said.

'Thing is, I'm having trouble with all the names already in place, never mind having to add another couple to the front. Brulee Duvalier Alexander de Morsay is quite a mouthful.'

'You cannot name a child after a dessert,' he said firmly.

'But I *can* name one after flowers, months of the year, stars, destinations, admirable qualities and the occasional fruit? How odd. And how about Hope?'

'No Hope whatsoever.'

'Serenity?'

'Unlikely,' he said.

'Unlikely's a little problematic, given all those last names. It could call her parentage into question and we wouldn't want that.'

Rafael shot her a speaking glance. He seemed a bit on edge today. He'd seemed a bit on edge ever since she'd fainted. Simone abandoned her teasing and headed for the truth of her thoughts on names for this child.

'My mother's name was Angelina,' she said tentatively. Her mother had died before Simone had reached her first year. Simone didn't remember her at all, she only knew *of* her. But what she knew sounded good. 'Angelina Grace.'

'That would work,' he said with a quiet smile that filled her heart.

'I've thought of a boy's name too.' She had, just now. In the interests of fairness and in the name of love. 'Harrison.'

'That would work too,' he said gruffly.

'I know. Now turn around, I'm on a roll.'

'No.'

He was staying away from her on purpose. He hadn't made love to her in two days. He'd held her gently through the night instead, as if afraid she would break. But the children of Caverness were not so easily broken. The children of Caverness refused to let despair get the better of them. The children of Caverness had ways. 'Do you remember the first time you kissed me?'

'Yes.'

'Not on my knee after I'd taken a tumble off the wall, or on the top of my head after we'd beaten Luc and Gabrielle at football.'

'Of course not,' he said with a tilt to his lips. 'Although for future reference I remember those times too.'

'It was at the harvest ball. And you were avoiding me for all you were worth.'

'Probably because I wasn't worth much.'

'You were to me.'

'I was parking cars, Simone. You were the belle of the ball.'

'It *was* a very nice car,' she said wistfully. 'Ferrari, wasn't it?'

'Bugatti.'

'Close enough.' By the time they'd finished with that first kiss he could have taken her anywhere, including on the bonnet. He hadn't. It had taken him another week to take her fully. Another week of restraint on his part and agonised waiting on hers. She hated waiting. 'I don't suppose you'd consider making love with me this morning?' she asked.

He looked as if he was considering it. His body certainly was. But he shook his head reluctantly. 'The doctor said three days of bed rest.'

'I'd just like to point out that what I have in mind is in fact a bed-based activity.'

He laughed at that, but he still shook his head. 'No.' He headed for the bathroom.

'Going somewhere?'

'The shower,' he said. 'And it had better be cold.'

'Want me to scrub your back for you?'

'I want you to eat your bread.'

'I've been thinking,' she said hurriedly, before he disappeared from her sight.

'I've noticed,' he said dryly.

Yes, well. Enforced bed rest did that to a person. 'Caverness's harvest ball is on in a couple of weeks. I'm thinking that if we arrive home in the next few days I'll be needing an escort and that you won't be parking cars. I'm thinking I'd like to do things properly this time.'

'You mean on the hood of the Bugatti?'

He *did* remember. Simone grinned. 'I mean that if a dark angel prince turned up bearing impure thoughts and blood red roses I could be persuaded to stay by his side.'

'For how long?' Rafe's wariness was back. It always came back when they talked of the future.

'That would depend,' she said gravely. 'On what the prince wants.'

CHAPTER TEN

'I STILL don't understand why you need a Bugatti by Friday,' said Gabrielle as they sat at their favourite café, and waited for their decaf to arrive, along with their day-old baguettes and, for Gabrielle, a side dish of olive and anchovy tapenade. Simone was trying her dry bread with Vegemite today, courtesy of a care package from Harrison.

'You know how when you were going to meet Luc in the caves you needed the right props?' said Simone. 'The white dress and your hair just so? Well, this is the same thing only I need a Bugatti.'

'Oh,' said Gabrielle. '*Oh*. Well, why didn't you say so? I thought you just wanted a car.'

'No, I'm aiming a little higher than that.'

'You mean an all-out war of seduction between you and Rafael?' said Gabrielle. 'Culminating in for ever and ever amen?'

'That's the plan.'

'I like it,' said Gabrielle. 'So you don't actually need to buy this car. You could just borrow one.'

'True,' said Simone thoughtfully. 'Although if everything goes according to plan it might be nice to have around the place. A little reminder, so to speak.'

'Trust me,' said Gabrielle. 'You do not need a Bugatti 101 as a reminder. Press a flower between the pages of a book or something.' Gabrielle scanned the pages of the antique car magazine spread out before her. 'Do you know how much one of these 1956 models *cost*?'

Simone peered over her water glass at the magazine spread out before Gabrielle. Gaby assisted by picking up the magazine and holding it out for her, with her finger pointing at the car in question. 'Oh,' said Simone. 'For *that*?'

'Yes,' said Gabrielle. 'For that. Seriously, could it get any uglier? No, you don't need to buy one of those. You need something borrowed. Does it have to be blue?'

'Only in that the Bugatti at the ball all those years ago was blue and I'd like to strive for authenticity,' said Simone.

'You do know that Josien kept attendance records of all the Harvest Balls,' said Gabrielle, leaning back in her chair with her fingers steepled in front of her. 'Not to mention a valet parking book recording which car arrived with whom and where the valets were supposed to put it?'

'*Did* she now?' said Simone.

'She *was* uncommonly thorough,' said Gabrielle, with the tiniest hint of pride. 'Put it this way, find that book, find the owner, a little finessing, a little persuasion, and you'll have yourself a blue Bugatti for the evening.'

'I like your thinking,' said Simone.

'What's not to like?' said Gabrielle. 'I've just saved you a fortune and preserved your sense of good taste as well.' Gabrielle leaned forward and looked at the picture once more. 'Seriously, who in their right mind would ever buy one of *those*?'

* * *

Luc and Rafael stood in the middle of the luxury antique car showroom and studied the models on offer. Most of them were pre 1950 models. Not all of them were driveable on today's roads.

'Seriously, Day, why a Bugatti?' asked Luc for approximately the fiftieth time. 'They're ugly, expensive, and worst of all designed by Italians although I will concede that the EB Veyron is quite a car. But these older ones…' Luc looked around him once more. 'How about a nice new tractor instead?'

'No. I need a Bugatti,' muttered Rafe, and nodded towards the big blue beast at the back of the showroom. '*That* Bugatti.'

The salesman had been hovering in the background. Crisp suit. Red tie. Receding hairline. Nice comb-over. Rafe caught his eye and he was with them in an instant. 'Tell me about the Bugatti 101,' he said.

'The 1956 model? What can I say?' said the salesman. '*Monsieur*, it's an *excellent* choice.'

Luc snorted. Rafe smiled at the salesman, unperturbed.

'All original parts, fully reconditioned engine, fully restored interior that comes with a ten-year guarantee—the interior's been done by our specialist master leather craftsman and is based on a truly inspired Hermès redesign—'

'How much?' Rafe cut through the salesman's homage to Hermès .

The salesman named a price that had Luc whooping with laughter and even the salesman smiling a little. 'And yet, it *is* a solid investment,' said the salesman. 'Particularly this model. There hasn't been a 1956 Bugatti 101 on the open market for over twenty years. There were only ever six of them made, as doubtless you already know. We're lucky to have it in the showroom. Luckier still to be representing the sale. *Messieurs*, I realise that the price sounds exorbitant, but this car truly is a rare collector's item.'

Rafe sighed. Why the hell couldn't Simone have cornered him when he'd been parking a Ferrari or a Lamborghini? Or even, heaven help him, something British like an Aston Martin? But no. 'Is it registered?' he said. 'Can we drive it?'

'It's car club registered,' said the salesman. 'And we can most certainly arrange for you to test-drive it at the current owner's private residence, for he does have race-track facilities. Of course, some sort of monetary expression of interest and good faith would be required.'

'Who owns it?' Luc had stopped laughing and started paying attention. 'I might know him.'

'*Monsieur*, I'm not at liberty to say,' replied the salesman. 'Although I can most certainly pass *your* names on to *him* at your request.'

Lucien gave his own name. The salesman's eyes widened. Lucien offered up Rafe's name as well and added a Prince to the front and a de Morsay de Maracey to the end.

'*Messieurs,*' said the salesman. 'Let me arrange that test-drive for you *now*.' He bowed low and scurried towards the tiny sales cubicle in the corner of the showroom just as fast as his soft salesman legs could carry him.

'Handy being a prince,' said Luc after a moment's thoughtful pause.

'Quite,' said Rafe, and then went and spoiled the surrealism of the moment with a shake of his head and a grin his face hadn't seen the likes of since childhood.

'Are you ever going to tell me *why* you want this monstrosity of a car?' asked Luc.

Rafe's smile widened. 'Never.'

The night of the harvest ball came complete with full moon, a starry sky and a Gabrielle who had taken over the duties of hostess for the evening in order to give Simone more time to plan her seduction of a certain prince who'd risen from her bed this morning and pranced around half-naked until she'd eaten a Vegemite rice cracker, at which point he'd kissed her on the temple and told her he'd see her this evening.

Both he and Luc had been noticeably absent all day. Guests would start arriving in another hour or so. Gabrielle currently paced Simone's room, a habit she'd likely as not picked up from her big brother. Gabrielle was, however, fully clothed—if you could call the backless and sleeveless midnight-blue ball gown and strappy diamanté sandals fully clothed.

'Luc said he'd be back at *five* at the latest,' Gabrielle murmured for the umpteenth time.

Simone glanced at her bedside clock. It was ten to seven.

'What did Rafe say?' asked Gabrielle next.

'Nothing.'

'Typical.' Gabrielle rolled her eyes. 'Okay, which one of us is going to call them?'

'You're the recently married woman,' said Simone. 'It's your *duty* to know where your husband is at all times. My guess is that Luc will think you remiss if you *don't* call him and find out what's going on.'

'You're right,' said Gabrielle and stopped her pacing. 'You're absolutely right. May I use your phone?'

'Of course.'

The conversation was short and sweet and consisted of, 'Where are you?' from Gabrielle, followed by her startled silence, then a bubbling giggle, and then the words, 'You're not serious?' Clearly Luc was serious because Gabrielle laughed again, told him he'd better be home within the hour, and hung up.

'Nicely done,' said Simone approvingly. 'Very wifely. So where are they?'

'About ten kilometres away. They're having car trouble.' Gabrielle sniggered again. 'One of the field hands is on his way with a trailer to collect them.'

Simone crossed to the dresser mirror and swiftly began to pin up her hair. Nine years ago Simone had worn a modest white gown to the harvest ball. She still had the gown, but it no longer accommodated her growing curves. Besides, she'd moved on from white.

Tonight's gown glowed boldly in the light, a deep royal red that flowed over her body like water and rippled with every move she made. The bodice was a halter-neck design and the seamstress had outdone herself when it came to making the alterations needed for a pregnant body and fuller breasts. Simone's shoes matched her dress and she planned on piling her hair high on her head and securing it with diamanté pins, mostly to afford Rafe the pleasure of taking it down.

She wore Duvalier diamonds in her ears and at her wrist, but she'd left her throat and her fingers bare. She would have Rafe's lips at her throat before the night was through, and that was all she needed.

Almost all she needed, she conceded. There was still the small matter of one day hearing three little words come out of Rafael's mouth.

Any order would do.

'Do you have a plan?' asked Gabrielle as she watched Simone pin up her hair.

'Not really.' All Simone had was her love and she'd been telegraphing that love as loudly as she could for weeks now. She'd never said it, not in so many words, because Rafe hadn't been ready to hear them. She hoped he was ready to hear them tonight. 'Get him to the Bugatti. Do a little reminiscing… Do you think it's wrong to propose to a man?'

'You're going to *propose* to Rafael tonight?'

'I'm not sure. I'm still thinking about it. But it's an option, right?'

'Well…' Gabrielle sounded somewhat conflicted.

'Because I've got this book.' Simone withdrew a slim leather bound volume of poems from her dresser drawer. 'I figure if I *am* going to do this I'll need some kind of lead in. I'm thinking about comparing him to a summer's day.'

Gabrielle ran her hand over her face, probably to camouflage the smile. 'Are you serious?'

'Well, I *was*. How about if I told him I loved him and then counted the ways?'

'I know how deep your love for my brother is, Simone. You'd be there all night.'

'Not if I followed the poem,' muttered Simone, leafing through the book for more inspiration.

'You could always wait,' said Gabrielle gently.

'I know.' Simone smoothed the pages of the book open unseeingly. 'It's just… I have a wonderful life, I know that. A child in my belly and the man I love by my side. I should be content. All the pieces of the puzzle fit exactly the way I want them to and the picture's so beautiful and full of light. There's just one piece missing, that's all. It's the piece where Rafael loves me, and I can't seem to find it and I don't know what to do.'

'Wait,' said Gabrielle gently. 'As far as I can see that's all you need to do now. Just wait, that's all, and trust Rafael to fight his way past his demons and through the briars to get to you. He's almost there. There aren't that many demons left. Returning to Caverness to face his memories of growing up here was one of the last and he's done it. For you,' said Gabrielle softly as she took the diamanté pin from Simone's fingers and positioned it in her hair. 'So if I were you, I would give him this night and simply love him and enjoy him the way you do and see where he takes you. He might just have found that last piece of the puzzle for you.'

Rafael and Luc got the Bugatti into place beneath the linden trees with half an hour to spare before the harvest ball guests were due to arrive. Luc cut out fast, muttering dire threats about torching Bugattis if his wife chewed him out for disappearing all day and turning up late for the ball.

Grimacing, Rafe fished his mobile from his pocket and dialled Gabrielle.

'We're here, we're late, and it's all my fault,' he said as soon as she answered. 'So be nice to your husband when he turns up because if you're not, he's going to torch my new car.'

'Where *is* your new car?' she asked lightly.

'Halfway down the linden drive. Why?'

'Does it run?' she said. 'Can you drive it?'

'After a fashion. It doesn't mind short distances.' It had managed the first twenty kilometres of a two-hundred-kilometre trip without stopping, hadn't it?

'Where are the keys?' she said next.

Rafael leaned down and looked in the car. No keys. He checked his pockets. No keys. Luc had been driving the monster the last time it had died. 'Luc has the keys,' he said.

'Oh, good,' she said.

'Do not let him torch my car.'

'Trust me,' she said, and hung up.

Rafael hit the chateau at full stride after that, in his quest to shower, shave and avoid Duvalier women until he was at least semi ready for this ball. Avoiding Simone was easier than expected for she was not in their room, although the lingering scent of her perfume was. Getting clean and dressed in under fifteen minutes was not a problem. Finding the little leather-bound book of poems that Etienne had given him proved impossible. Still, he did have the frog he'd scoured the Caverness water gardens for at dawn this morning. Handy things to have around, frogs.

He'd deposited the tiny creature in an upturned ter-racotta flowerpot in the window box just outside their room, figuring it would be safe there for the day. He gently lifted the pot. Nothing. He looked *in* the pot. No frog. It had probably dug into the soil for the night. Never mind. Rafe had applied a modicum of forward thinking and had a back-up plan when it came to am-phibians. Fortunately, Cartier made platinum frogs for people just like him, and smothered them in emeralds and diamonds and hung them from filigree chains. Go figure.

He found *that* frog in his sock drawer and slipped it into his jacket pocket. What else did he need tonight?

Courage, he needed that.

Confidence, he would need that too.

Trust.

Trust was the kicker. Could he entrust his heart to the Duvalier princess as he'd entrusted it once before?

With every sun-filled day and passion-filled night with Simone, the answer became even more blindingly obvious.

Yes.

Rafe found the House of Duvalier heiress in the kitchen overseeing last-minute food and beverage preparations for the ball. She looked up and saw him and her eyes warmed in welcome. She looked every inch the princess tonight; a vibrant, accomplished woman with a radiance about her that put all other women to shame. Pregnancy suited her as Chateau des Caverness suited her and Rafael knew that he'd made no mistake in bringing her home.

She'd have stayed with him in Maracey. She would stay with him in Maracey again and set every one of Etienne's statesman aflutter with her scheming on his behalf, but for now Caverness was where she needed to be and this was where they would stay.

Rafe sent his heiress a crooked smile as plates and glassware clattered around them. Someone dropped a fork. Someone else sighed. Simone smiled wryly and crossed to his side.

'You have no idea of the havoc you wreak when you smile like that, do you?' she said when she reached him.

He smiled again, just so he could watch her eyes darken. 'Oh, I have *some* idea,' he murmured, and set his lips to her cheek in greeting. 'Evening, princess.' Anything more would have to wait until they were alone.

He hated waiting.

'Walk with me in the garden,' he said as she preceded him from the bustling kitchen, and, wrapping her arm around his waist and tucking in close to his heart, she did.

He hated hard, did Rafael. It was a flaw in his nature and he knew it full well. But he loved hard too and he'd never stopped loving this woman, not once in ten long years. It was time he made that clear to her.

'Gabrielle and I planned a surprise for you,' she said as they strolled along the wide stone walkway towards the steps that would lead them to the formal front gardens that had been lit for the evening by hundreds of glowing garden candles. Caverness could shine when it wanted to, he remembered that about it now, and tonight someone had gone all out to see that it did. 'We were all set to reveal it to you this afternoon only you weren't around.'

'Luc and I did have one or two unexpected delays throughout the day.' Or ten. 'May I have my surprise now?'

'No, you're going to have to wait for the ball now, though I can tell you what it is.'

Rafe smiled as he took her hand and guided her down the steps. She *wanted* to tell him. She was busting to tell him. 'Tell me.'

'Harrison's here. He'll be here for two weeks. Gabrielle can't stop hugging him she's so excited. She's already planning to take him on a tour of Hammer-schmidt tomorrow. I said we'd join them.'

'Good.' Rafe had been helping Luc rip out old grape-vines and prepare new ground for new rootstock. He and Luc worked well together and always had and Rafe was more than willing to offer his labour in the hope of getting the property ready for Duvalier occupation before small babies arrived.

'We should take something along to plant in the garden there,' murmured Simone. 'A cutting from Caverness. A reminder.' She slanted him a glance from solemn eyes. 'Does it bother you being back here?'

'Not as much as I thought it would,' he murmured. 'It's different now. *I'm* different.' They'd reached the bottom of the stairs. 'I caught a frog for you this morning. But I lost it in the window box.'

'Tell Ruby,' said Simone with a grin. 'She'll find it for you.'

'They were never really frogs, you know,' he said, wishing like hell he'd found that blasted book of poems. 'They just looked like frogs, hopped like frogs and lived like frogs.'

'So what were they?' she murmured. 'Princes?'

'They were pieces of my heart,' he said gruffly, and shoved his at her feet. He dug into his pocket for the emerald frog and held it out towards her. 'It's the last piece,' he said. 'I gave the rest of it to you bit by bit.'

He watched in silence as the moisture in Simone's eyes threatened to overflow, but she took the little frog from him and held it up to the light of the harvest moon. Not that she could see it for the waterworks, but for once he didn't mind a woman's tears. 'I love it,' she said. 'I love *you*, Rafael Alexander, whoever you are, and I always have. I've been wanting to tell you ever since you turned up in my garden and demanded I come with you to Maracey. I've been waiting for you to notice.'

Rafael smiled and let her words of love fill him. 'I'm a little slow on the uptake sometimes.'

'I forgive you,' she said magnanimously. 'You had a lot on your mind. A future to consider. A past to reconcile.' She offered him a solemn smile. 'All that has shaped you, and all that you are. It's not easy, sometimes, to get you to drop your guard.'

Rafe knew her statement for truth. 'It's down now. For you.'

'I know.' Simone separated the strands of the filigree chain and put the frog to her neck. 'It's a situation I intend to take full advantage of for the rest of my life.'

He loved a canny princess.

'Walk with me,' she said, and pointed towards the garages and gardening sheds that flanked one side of the chateau. 'There's something I want to show you.'

'And I, you,' he said. He gestured towards the linden-tree drive. 'Only it's that way.'

A rapping noise sounded from high above, a determined fist upon a window pane. The window opened, and Gabrielle Duvalier, mistress of Caverness, leaned out. Lucien Duvalier, the master of Caverness, leaned out too.

'Nice frog,' Luc told his sister. 'It's very you.' He shot Rafe an amused glance. 'The prince suits you too, although I abhor his taste in cars.'

'Are you going for a walk?' asked Gabrielle, and without waiting for their reply pointed towards the caves of Caverness, where vignerons had been storing their wines for centuries. 'I strongly recommend that you wander on into the south storage cave.' She disappeared, only to return to the window moments later with something in her hand. 'You'll need keys to get in.' She tossed them down to Rafael. 'You should go straight there. Detours at this particular point in time are only going to scare you.' Gabrielle blew them a cheeky kiss. '*Bon soir,*' she said, and then the window pane slid down and she and Luc disappeared.

Rafe jingled the keys in his hand. Simone smiled up

at him. 'Do you know why she wants us to head for the caves?' asked Simone.

'Not exactly.' But he could guess. Gabrielle had been aware of the potential need for privacy when gifting Simone with a Bugatti. Gabrielle had arranged for the Bugatti to be shifted to a location that would ensure such privacy. Gabrielle was extremely good at forward thinking and paving his way with puppies and now privacy. Rafe really needed to do something wonderful for her in return. Maybe he could get her a horse.

'Shall we?' he said.

Simone slanted her angel a sideways glance. She put her hand on his arm to steady herself and removed first one ruby-red stiletto and then the other and looped the straps over Rafael's fingers.

'Do you remember the *way* to the south storage cave?' she asked archly. 'I know what your memory's like.'

'Happens I do,' he murmured with one of those rare smiles that could light up a day, or a sweet harvest night.

Simone flashed him a smile as she bent down and bunched up the skirt of her gown until it was thigh-high. Rafe's eye's widened. His grin grew wolfish. 'Race you,' she said, and took to her heels.

Rafe caught her well before they reached the caves, and caught her hand and kept right on running until locked cave doors blocked their progress. Gasping for breath and laughing with joy, Simone leaned against the wall while Rafe opened the door to the tunnel that led to the south storage caves. 'You might want to lock it behind you,' she suggested.

'I do want to lock it behind me,' he said as they slipped inside. He shut the door behind them and hauled her up against him as he ensured their privacy. 'The baby,' he muttered as his body responded to her proximity with satisfying speed.

'Is going to be a runner,' she said as Rafe's bow tie headed south, and then his jacket, and then the buttons of his shirt came undone beneath her questing fingers. 'Possibly a stripper.'

'Definitely a handful,' he said as he captured her mouth and catapulted her into the stars.

'Do we really need to go all the way to the south cave?' Simone was quite happy to take matters in hand right here, right now, although a surface other than the floor would definitely be an asset.

'Maybe they put a bed in there,' he murmured. 'Looks like they left us some champagne.' He glanced towards the tiny side bench by the door and Simone followed his gaze. Two champagne flutes sat on the bench and beside them stood a silver ice bucket with two bottles in it, up to their necks in ice. She wriggled free of Rafe and went to investigate. One was a bottle of 1956 Chateau Caverness. The other was a bottle of Perrier.

'That's just sad,' she said.

Rafe picked up the ice bucket and the glasses, heaven knew where he'd left her shoes, and headed down the tunnel. 'They're very thorough,' he said. 'My hopes of a bed are improving.'

They headed for the storage cavern Gabrielle had suggested. It was one of their bigger caverns and usually functioned as a collection point for orders. There were dozens of secluded and romantic nooks and nestlings in the labyrinth that made up the caves of Caverness. The south storage cave was not one of them. Even the tunnel they walked along was one of the main

thoroughfares, capable of admitting forklifts and electronically powered carts that towed trailers full of
champagne to the outside world.

They reached the cavern and stopped. Simone snickered. Rafael blinked.

Two butt-ugly blue Bugattis sat side by side in the
middle of the empty cave, their bumpers almost touching, and their chrome bits gleaming in the soft light of
dozens upon dozens of tiny candles.

'I love my family,' murmured Simone. 'Which
one's yours?'

'The one on the right,' he murmured. 'Please don't
tell me you bought the one on the left.' He sounded as
if he were in pain.

'Of course not,' she said. 'I borrowed it from the
Comte d'Aredeney. It's going back tomorrow. When's
yours going back?'

Silence.

Simone turned her head to stare at him. 'You didn't.'

'Think of it as an investment,' he said a touch desperately.

Simone began to smile. Then she began to laugh. 'In
what?'

'In our future, not to mention a reminder of some
very good times in our past.'

Simone approached Rafael's car and opened the rear
door wide. 'After you,' she said.

But Rafael hadn't finished yet. 'I have this puppy,'
he said. 'And, and…ducks!' She stood there, his wanton
princess, with her hair falling around her face and her
eyes bright with love and he forgot all about the list of
things he felt he could offer her and went straight to the
heart of the matter. 'And a need for you that burns so
deep inside me it hurts.' He took a breath and to hell

with love poems. 'Marry me,' he said. 'There's this guest house that's perfect for weddings. Friendly reception. Good restaurant service. Fine winery nearby. There's this garden between the restaurant and the guest house and halfway between the two there's this nook that's perfect for—'

'Rafael,' she said imperiously. 'I'll marry you. Please, just get in the car.'

But he hadn't finished yet. 'When?'

'Soon,' she said. 'Even sooner if you'd just get in the car. I'll marry you now if you want me to, in front of a pair of Bugattis and with God as my witness. I love you. I've never stopped loving you. And you might as well make yourself comfortable,' she said as she removed her remaining hairpins and let her hair tumble free. 'Because I do intend to count the ways.'

* * * * *

*Harlequin Intrigue top author Delores Fossen
presents a brand-new series of
breathtaking romantic suspense!*
TEXAS MATERNITY: HOSTAGES
The first installment available May 2010:
THE BABY'S GUARDIAN

Shaw cursed and hooked his arm around Sabrina.

Despite the urgency that the deadly gunfire created, he tried to be careful with her, and he took the brunt of the fall when he pulled her to the ground. His shoulder hit hard, but he held on tight to his gun so that it wouldn't be jarred from his hand.

Shaw didn't stop there. He crawled over Sabrina, sheltering her pregnant belly with his body, and he came up ready to return fire.

This was obviously a situation he'd wanted to avoid at all cost. He didn't want his baby in the middle of a fight with these armed fugitives, but when they fired that shot, they'd left him no choice. Now, the trick was to get Sabrina safely out of there.

"Get down," someone on the SWAT team yelled from the roof of the adjacent building.

Shaw did. He dropped lower, covering Sabrina as best he could.

There was another shot, but this one came from a rifleman on the SWAT team. Shaw didn't look up, but he heard the sound of glass being blown apart.

The shots continued, all coming from his men, which meant it might be time to try to get Sabrina to better cover. Shaw glanced at the front of the building.

So that Sabrina's pregnant belly wouldn't be smashed against the ground, Shaw eased off her and moved her to a sitting position so that her back was against the brick wall. They were close. Too close. And face-to-face.

He found himself staring right into those sea-green eyes.

How will Shaw get Sabrina out?
Follow the daring rescue and the heartbreaking
aftermath in THE BABY'S GUARDIAN
by Delores Fossen,
available May 2010 from Harlequin Intrigue.

HARLEQUIN *Presents*

Bestselling Harlequin Presents® author

Lynne Graham

introduces

VIRGIN ON HER WEDDING NIGHT

Valente Lorenzatto never forgave Caroline Hales's
abandonment of him at the altar. But now he's
made millions and claimed his aristocratic Venetian
birthright—and he's poised to get his revenge.
He'll ruin Caroline's family by buying out their
company and throwing them out of their mansion...
unless she agrees to give him the wedding night
she denied him five years ago....

**Available May 2010
from Harlequin Presents!**

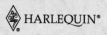
HARLEQUIN®

INTRIGUE®

BESTSELLING
HARLEQUIN INTRIGUE® AUTHOR

DELORES FOSSEN

PRESENTS AN ALL-NEW
THRILLING TRILOGY

TEXAS MATERNITY: HOSTAGES

When masked gunmen take over the maternity ward at a San Antonio hospital, local cops, FBI and the scared mothers can't figure out any possible motive. Before long, secrets are revealed, and a city that has been on edge since the siege began learns the truth behind the negotiations and must deal with the fallout.

LOOK FOR

THE BABY'S GUARDIAN, May
DEVASTATING DADDY, June
THE MOMMY MYSTERY, July

REQUEST YOUR
FREE BOOKS!

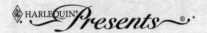 

2 FREE NOVELS PLUS
2 FREE GIFTS!

YES! Please send me 2 FREE Harlequin Presents® novels and my 2 FREE gifts (gifts are worth about $10). After receiving them, if I don't wish to receive any more books, I can return the shipping statement marked "cancel." If I don't cancel, I will receive 6 brand-new novels every month and be billed just $4.05 per book in the U.S. or $4.74 per book in Canada. That's a saving of close to 15% off the cover price! It's quite a bargain! Shipping and handling is just 50¢ per book in the U.S. and 75¢ per book in Canada.* I understand that accepting the 2 free books and gifts places me under no obligation to buy anything. I can always return a shipment and cancel at any time. Even if I never buy another book, the two free books and gifts are mine to keep forever.

106 HDN E4FN   306 HDN E4FY

Name _____ (PLEASE PRINT)

Address _____ Apt. #

City _____ State/Prov. _____ Zip/Postal Code

Signature (if under 18, a parent or guardian must sign)

Mail to the **Harlequin Reader Service:**
IN U.S.A.: P.O. Box 1867, Buffalo, NY 14240-1867
IN CANADA: P.O. Box 609, Fort Erie, Ontario L2A 5X3

Not valid for current subscribers to Harlequin Presents books.

Are you a current subscriber to Harlequin Presents books and want to receive the larger-print edition? Call 1-800-873-8635 today!

* Terms and prices subject to change without notice. Prices do not include applicable taxes. N.Y. residents add applicable sales tax. Canadian residents will be charged applicable provincial taxes and GST. Offer not valid in Quebec. This offer is limited to one order per household. All orders subject to approval. Credit or debit balances in a customer's account(s) may be offset by any other outstanding balance owed by or to the customer. Please allow 4 to 6 weeks for delivery. Offer available while quantities last.

Your Privacy: Harlequin Books is committed to protecting your privacy. Our Privacy Policy is available online at www.eHarlequin.com or upon request from the Reader Service. From time to time we make our lists of customers available to reputable third parties who have a product or service of interest to you. If you would prefer we not share your name and address, please check here. ☐

Help us get it right—We strive for accurate, respectful and relevant communications. To clarify or modify your communication preferences, visit us at www.ReaderService.com/consumerschoice.

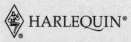
HARLEQUIN®

American ★ Romance®

LAURA MARIE ALTOM

The Baby Twins

Stephanie Olmstead has her hands full raising
her twin baby girls on her own. When she runs
into old friend Brady Flynn, she's shocked to find
herself suddenly attracted to the handsome airline
pilot! Will this flyboy be the perfect daddy—
or will he crash and burn?

Babies
&
Bachelors
USA

"LOVE, HOME & HAPPINESS"

www.eHarlequin.com

HAR75309

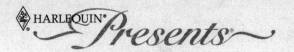

Coming Next Month

in **Harlequin Presents® EXTRA.** Available April 13, 2010.

#97 RICH, RUTHLESS AND SECRETLY ROYAL
Robyn Donald
Regally Wed

#98 FORGOTTEN MISTRESS, SECRET LOVE-CHILD
Annie West
Regally Wed

#99 TAKEN BY THE PIRATE TYCOON
Daphne Clair
Ruthless Tycoons

#100 ITALIAN MARRIAGE: IN NAME ONLY
Kathryn Ross
Ruthless Tycoons

Coming Next Month

in **Harlequin Presents®.** Available April 27, 2010:

#2915 VIRGIN ON HER WEDDING NIGHT
Lynne Graham

#2916 TAMED: THE BARBARIAN KING
Jennie Lucas
Dark-Hearted Desert Men

#2917 BLACKWOLF'S REDEMPTION
Sandra Marton
Men Without Mercy

#2918 THE PRINCE'S CHAMBERMAID
Sharon Kendrick
At His Service

#2919 MISTRESS: PREGNANT BY THE SPANISH BILLIONAIRE
Kim Lawrence

#2920 RUTHLESS RUSSIAN, LOST INNOCENCE
Chantelle Shaw